The Kingdom of Chaos

Becoming Fae

J.J. Smeck

THE LOST KINGDOM

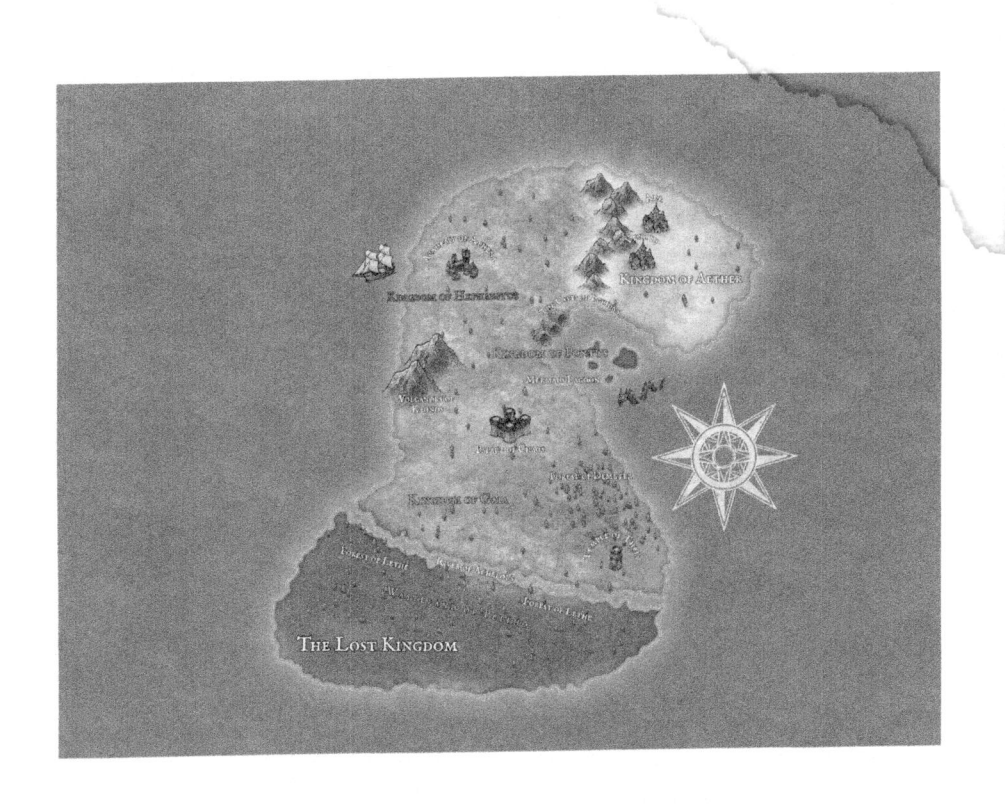

Contents

Title Page	
Chapter 1	1
Chapter 2	5
Chapter 3	21
Chapter 4	35
Chapter 5	45
Chapter 6	54
Chapter 7	57
Chapter 8	62
Chapter 9	71
Chapter 10	75
Chapter 11	83
Chapter 12	90
Chapter 13	96
Chapter 14	101
Chapter 15	109
Chapter 16	118
Chapter 17	132
Chapter 18	149
Chapter 19	154

About The Author	161
Books In This Series	163

Chapter 1

I sluggishly roused to the sound of a slow drip against a hard floor. My head was pounding, and a shiver ran down my spine as I took in the damp, dark room around me. I was lying on a cobblestone floor that felt as cold as ice, so cold it burned my skin. This wasn't right. I slowly raised myself on my arm, but pain shot through me, and I winced. The sudden movement of my face caused even more pain, and I gingerly reached up to feel that one eye felt slightly swollen. As I took in the small size of the stone chamber, I lurched up to a sitting position. The pain continued to assault me, and I looked down to find small cuts and bruises covering most of my body. What the hell had happened to me? My head swam with confusion, and I had to fight the all-consuming feeling of sleep trying to wash over me.

My mind jogged to catch up with my reality, as I tried to think of what I'd been doing before this moment. As I looked down at my thin chemise, bits and pieces started to fall together like a distorted puzzle. On the eve of my twenty-first birthday, I had gone to bed in the small cottage that I shared with my father. I had been excited to wake up the next day and accept my fate and the gift of my elemental affinities. Every Fae awoke on their twenty-first birthday with their abilities revealed to them. I had barely slept all week due to the anticipation of what form I would be able to shift into. I was born in the Kingdom of Aether, the northern territory of the royal Kingdom of Chaos, so I knew I would be able to harness the elemental affinity of air. Well, I hoped I would be able to harness air. Some Fae were gifted with the power of multiple regions, but I had ruled that out as a possibility since my father was half-mortal. In fact, I wasn't even sure if I would be gifted with any abilities at all, which was the cause of my anxiety and anticipation.

As luck would have it, I had spent my last powerless night alone. My father meant well but was a slave to his addictions, namely gambling, and alcohol. Just a week ago, he had been hauled off to answer for his crimes. I knew that upon turning twenty-one, I could inquire about his penalties at the small prison north of town and attempt to free my father. Unfortunately for my father, that wasn't my first priority this morning and certainly wasn't now that I was lying on a cold, stone floor alone and injured.

The room I was in had no windows, so I had no idea if it was day or night. I had no idea how long I had been unconscious, so I was left with an overwhelming sense of confusion. I had a feeling that it must be after midnight, and if so, my powers, if I had any, may have formed in my body. I delicately held out my hands in front of me, favoring my injured arm. Unsure of how to activate my powers, I closed my eyes and attempted to force out a mental command. I looked down at my hands, and a frown creased my face as I realized nothing was happening. That wasn't right, and I began to grow concerned. Maybe it wasn't, in fact, past midnight? Or perhaps someone had carried me across the lines of another court. A Fae could only wield their power in the Kingdom where their citizenship belonged initially, and as I was unawakened, my powers would not work anywhere other than the Kingdom of Aether. But who would carry me across territory lines? Who would kidnap me at all? And why on the eve of my twenty-first birthday? Was someone trying to stop me from awakening my power? Who the hell would care? I was no one special and had no money or anything of value to offer them. My mind raced with the possibilities - searching for answers and coming up empty.

After a few moments of staring at my trembling hands with panic rising in my chest, I took a moment to think of how

I would get myself out of this room. I searched the darkness, looking around for an exit and froze when I heard the shifting metallic sound of armor outside a wooden door that blended into the darkness so well that I hadn't noticed it yet. I heard heavy steps approaching. I slowly laid back down in case they were coming for me, hoping they would believe I was still unconscious. An unfamiliar man's booming voice rang out in the silence. "Is she ready to move?" he said with a gruff voice that sounded irritated and impatient.

My heart started beating wildly. Move me? I closed my eyes, pretending to be asleep, as two sets of armor clinking drew closer to the door. Who the fuck would be interested in capturing me? And where were they moving me? I had never strayed far from home. As I silently panicked, I started searching my mind for any reason they may have to be interested in my capture.

I was an average girl, but not because I wasn't sharp-witted. I was bored and unmotivated. Without a constant parental figure, I would just kind of coast through life, doing as I please. When my father wasn't around to help provide for our household, I stole from the local market. I would casually walk through the busy market stalls with my basket and fill it item by item as I brushed past their stands. Would a local vendor go to such lengths to punish me for my thieving? While possible, I had been pretty careful, and not many people would have noticed my sleight of hand.

I wasn't some little prim and proper maiden. I was rough around the edges, built from a lack of parental supervision and evenings spent in a tavern with my father. I loved my father, but he didn't really have an effect, good or bad, on my life anymore. The other local children bullied me for being poor. I sometimes stole my own clothes and "borrowed" what I needed from classmates. Since completing my required academic years, I stole when the opportunity presented itself.

The occasional times I got caught stealing in the market, I fought my way out of it. I never stole anything on a large scale, just what I needed when desperate. I had to be willing to fight for myself because who else would? I only had one living relative that I knew of: my drunkard father. I prided myself in taking care of myself and fighting my own battles.

I snapped myself out of my wandering thoughts back to the present moment. I had to figure out what was going on and how to get myself out of this situation quickly. No one was coming to rescue me. No one even knew I was missing. I could disappear, and no one, but my unreliable drunkard father, would be the wiser. As it was, I was used to taking care of myself and my father at times.

This situation would be no different.

Chapter 2

The door swung open. I continued to lay on the floor, pretending to be unconscious. The males shuffled to either side of me while their armor clamored. Their large bodies filled the room as they tried to approach me on either side scuffing against the wall. The first male grabbed me up under my arm and hoisted me up to a standing position sending pain searing through my limb. The other male grabbed my other arm and leaned forward under my arm, shouldering half my weight. I gasped, confirming to the males that I was awake and aware.

"Who are you? Where are you taking me?" I choked out nervously. I made a weak attempt to thrash out of their hold as I felt pain and soreness in every inch of my body. I might be in a precarious situation, but I would not go down without a fight.

Neither male answered, nor seemed to struggle against my attempts to get loose. They started to drag me out of the room and into the narrow hallway. Their weight pressed in on both sides of me, reminding me how bruised and damaged I was. Once I crossed the threshold of the door, a third armored male thrust something onto my hands. I looked down to see leather gloves covering my hands and wrists. They were black and had a metallic circular design across the back of them that continued down each finger. I could only assume this was to stop me from using my elemental affinities. Little did they know, I didn't even know what I could harness or if I had any abilities at all. The male stepped aside, into a neighboring cell to allow for more room in the cramped hallway, and I was shoved down the hall by the two armored males on either side. When we reached the end of the hall, there was a stone stairwell that led up to a large wooden door. The wooden door was opened by someone from the outside and the wind flung it the rest of the way open until it banged against the wall.

We emerged into a windy, dark night where three dark blue carriages were waiting with six more armored guards. I still could not determine what time it was, let alone what day. My eyes roamed over the scene, taking in all the details so I could start making sense of everything. I had always been extremely observant, which is what made me an excellent thief. I noticed things others didn't. I watched people without them even noticing me. Most other people seemed to go through life oblivious to what was going on around them - or, who was creeping up on them and taking advantage of their absent-mindedness.

The carriages were made of wood and had curtained windows so I couldn't see inside. On top of their natural wood color, it was painted a dark blue with gold trim. The paint was new, but the carriages appeared to be a little run down. The wheels were splintering slightly, and I could tell the wood was scuffing in some places. There were two horses leading each carriage and behind them was a bench for the drivers. The horses' reins were ordinary brown leather and were decidedly plain next to the ornamental richness of the rest of the carriage. Odd.

We took four or five steps out of the open door and approached the second carriage. As we approached, the door swung open, and out stepped a male that looked like royalty. He was tall, somewhat muscular, and clean-cut. His shoulders were broad, and he looked as though he was someone of importance. He wore a formal coat with the royal colors of the Kingdom of Pontus, more commonly known as the Water Realm. Forcing my gaze from him, I looked at the emblem on the side of the carriage. There I found a circle with a picture of the god of Pontus. Returning my gaze to him, I found the same emblem on the right breast pocket of his coat. His realm followed the views of the God, Pontus, the God of the sea. Those with water magic, and those who hoped to obtain water magic, lived there. Looking closely at the carriage I could see the emblem had a small picture of Pontus, a bearded man with two crab claw horns atop his head.

Why would someone capture me, in the dead of night, on the eve of my twenty-first birthday and bring me to the fucking Water Realm?

"Evelyn, do you know why you are here?" he asked, interrupting my thoughts. I snapped my eyes back to his face. Before I could open my mouth to speak, he snapped at the guards, "Why in Hades does she look so... abused?" Thanks, I guess? Not what I hoped to hear when meeting an important, slightly attractive Fae male who seemed to be in control of my future.

The guard at my right opened his mouth to speak but before a word came out, he dropped to the ground in a crumpled heap - instantly dead. I was completely shocked and confused. I realized my mouth was now hanging open and I quickly shut it. I looked up from the body next to me and into the face of the male before me. He had his palms outstretched in front of him. One palm was aimed toward the male on the ground and the other one was fixed on the remaining guard. He slowly twisted his hand, drawing his fingers into a tight fist. The male beside me seemed to tense and respond with a groan. The male's rough voice filled the air while his palms remained outstretched. "Speak Tifton," he commanded.

The remaining guard at my side responded nervously, "Sire, I apologize. She was quite powerful. She was able to fight us even once we had put a demobilizing spell on her." He was now kneeling on the rocky ground and his head drooped low in a bow. He looked back up out of the top of his eyes. I looked at his face and saw a split on the top of his nose and discoloration under one of his eyes. That did look like something I had done but I had no recollection of it.

My mind started whirling. "Sire"? This male before me must be a part of the royal family of Pontus. I was not one for politics and my father certainly did not keep me abreast on the royal lines in the other three Kingdoms. I knew the current King, Finlin, and Queen, Annabell, of the royal Kingdom of Chaos, the Royal Empire of the continent, but that was the extent of my knowledge. In fact, I only knew their names and nothing else about them really. They controlled the entire continent and oversaw the four smaller Kingdoms. The royal Kingdom of Chaos was broken down into four Kingdoms, previously five, divided by elemental realms, and each was ruled by a Lord and Lady. The Air Realm was referred to as the Kingdom of Aether, where my citizenship lies. There, the citizens harness the elemental affinity of air. To the west, was the Light Realm, the Kingdom of Hephaestus. Its citizens harnessed the elemental affinity of light and could create fire, speak with the stars, and manipulate light and heat. On the eastern side of the continent, along the coast, was the Water Realm, the Kingdom of Pontus. Their citizens harnessed the elemental affinity of water and could shift into different water creatures. South of Pontus, was the Earth Realm, called the Kingdom of Gaia. The citizens there could harness the elemental affinity of the earth, manipulating plants and the Earth's surface. The southernmost tip of the continent was where the Lost Realm, the Kingdom of the Lost, used to be. It was said to have been desolate and abandoned for the last fifty years.

I also knew that each realm has a royal court, under the Lord and Lady. The court consisted of ten Fae who served as part of the governing body with all decisions lying with the Lord or Lady. I hadn't been particularly interested in politics and now I wanted to kick myself. That knowledge surely would have come in handy now.

The male in front of me barked, making me jump. "Those were not your instructions. Your instructions were to bring her to me unharmed," he said, furiously. Quickly, he released the invisible hold he had on the guard and dropped his hand to his side. The guard crumpled to the ground, clearly dead as well. My weight became my own to support and, realizing how sore I was, I felt weak and small standing here on my own. I sucked in a breath trying to combat the pain. My eyes were wide as I realized how quickly and effortlessly he had ended those two full-grown males.

The male looked at me and said, "The Lord wants you transported safely. You were in danger once your powers surfaced at midnight. The protection spell could no longer keep you hidden." My eyes slowly returned to their normal size. If this male was on my side then, surely, I wasn't in danger of an instant death like the two males now laying on the dark, rocky ground.

It took me a second to respond as I searched the male's face for emotion. He looked anxious and concerned. Was he confused about who was standing before him? I tried not to sound like a naive child when I responded, "And who is it that you think I am?". Hopefully, this was just a mix-up and I could be returned home.

He laughed lightly, "Evelyn, we really don't have time for games." His gaze raked from my eyes over my body in the thin chemise and down to my toes. I suddenly felt exposed and perplexed. He drug his eyes back up to meet mine again and my face flushed at his casual tone and indecent gaze. I cocked my head to one side trying to think. I had no memory of this male and suddenly I didn't feel safe with him anymore.

How did he know my name? Maybe he thought he knew who I was but he certainly had me confused with someone else. Typically my friends called me by my nickname, Evie, and not by my given name of Evelyn. In fact, I don't think anybody had ever called me Evelyn, not that I would have minded it.

He gestured for me to get in the carriage before us with a slight jerk of his head and said, "Please, come sit down in the carriage so we can begin our journey, Evelyn." He held his hand out to help me in. I took a few hesitant steps forward, my nerves settling, as I realized that this male didn't want to hurt me. As my nerves calmed, I became aware of how cold I suddenly was... and how little I was wearing. I had on a thin, white nightgown that buttoned down the front and hung just above my knees. The wind was strong and blew the nightgown tightly against my body, revealing my curves through the nearly translucent fabric. My long brown hair was flying wildly around my head in the breeze. I cringed when I thought about how I must look right now to this male.

As I approached the carriage, the guard next to it caught my eye. I did a double-take. He was taller than the first male and he had jet black hair. He had strong, prominent features and was far more muscular than the original male too with his muscles straining against his coat and shirt. He clenched his jaw, drawing my attention to his sharp cheekbones and hard jawline. He was incredibly attractive. Time slowed as he cut his gaze to mine and we made eye contact. His bright green eyes glistened and the wind blew his black hair. I had a feeling in my stomach similar to that of falling off a cliff. I felt like he was trying to tell me something with his eyes but the meaning was just beyond my grasp. My lips parted slightly and his gaze flicked from my lips then back to my eyes, all in slow motion. I closed my mouth and swallowed.

As I got closer to the male that was providing me with safe travel, the guard's eyes followed me. Time was still passing in slow motion and my body moved as if I was walking through thick mud. Suddenly, I felt an odd spark of lightning travel through my entire body. It started in my chest and worked its way quickly down to my toes and through my extremities. It strengthened as it shot out into each of my limbs and returned to my center traveling back to my chest. It happened so fast and was over so quickly, that I thought that I might have imagined it. Perhaps I was going into some kind of shock at the events over the last few hours. Once the lightning zapped through my body, I was left feeling chilled to the bone. It was a strange sensation. It didn't feel like a chill due to the strong wind, but an inward cold like I missed the lightning's presence and warmth. I shivered lightly and my teeth chattered together uncontrollably.

Realizing I must be standing in front of the first male now, I broke the guard's gaze and time returned to its normal pace. The male's hand was out, offering to help me into the carriage. When I lifted my hand he saw the thick leather gloves that had been shoved onto my hands and sighed. "Here let me help you get those off," he said. "I apologize for your treatment, Evelyn. They took their loyalty to the Kingdom a little too far."

"Please, call me Evie," I interjected. He gave a small smile in acknowledgment.

He pointed his palms at my gloved hands and said, "Removere." The gloves instantly disappeared. Then he leaned in close, "Sana," he whispered, brushing his fingers lightly over my cheek. As he did, my pain started to ebb away and I could feel my eye returning to its normal size. I saw the black-haired guard shift his weight from one foot to the other out of the corner of my eye.

The male held out his hand and I took it with one of mine, using my other hand to hold my nightgown down as I walked up the two small wooden steps into the carriage and lowered myself into the backward-facing seat. As I sat, my nightgown shifted up my thighs, exposing the skin above my knees. The male climbed in once I was seated and dropped down into the seat across from me. The door was shut, cutting off the loud noise created by the strong wind outside.

We sat a few feet apart, with our knees almost grazing each

other. As he settled into his seat, he attempted to raise his gaze to meet mine, but it seemed to snag on my chest. I looked down surprised. The top three buttons of my nightgown must've come unbuttoned during the scuffle I had with the guards. I was revealing significantly more of my body than I normally would have at my first meeting with a gentleman. I wouldn't consider myself a prude, and I certainly wasn't lacking experience, but I did make males work to bed me. And here I sat in a thin, unbuttoned nightgown, crawling up my thighs, leaving little to the imagination. Albeit, it was a dirty nightgown that matched my dirty skin and wild hair. I must've looked unsightly.

I cleared my throat and his gaze shot to my face. "Are there more appropriate clothes for me for such a journey?" I asked with a slight tremble in my tone.

He jumped slightly, as if in a trance himself. "Oh, yes, Evelyn. I do apologize. I will step out of the carriage to let you get changed." He stood swiftly to exit the carriage. A cold rush of air entered as he opened the door, then shut it abruptly. I looked across the carriage and saw a neatly folded stack of clothes there. I quickly changed into a tight pair of pants, a long, thin sweater, and a pair of boots I recognized as my own. Where had these come from? There was also a traveling coat and I slipped it over my shoulders. I was still trying to warm up from being outside. My skin stung a little. I felt warmer already but still felt cold inside from where the lightning had traveled through my body.

I cracked the door to see the male standing with his back to the carriage looking out into the dark of night. He stood next to the guard with black hair and bright green eyes. Their heads were leaning close together as they spoke quietly.

"I am finished changing," I said, still confused about this journey. I felt confident that I was no longer traveling as a criminal. A criminal would not be given a change of clothes and made to travel in a carriage with a male with some sort of royal position.

The male turned at the hips to hear what I was saying. Once I had finished speaking, he called over his shoulder, "I'll be just a moment."

"Jake, we will be at our destination in a week or so," he finished speaking to the guard, loud enough for me to hear. "We have to make a stop along the way that I will explain more about when we get closer," he added.

He turned on his feet to face me, then climbed back into the carriage to sit across from me once again. Guards headed in different directions around the outside of the carriage. I had noticed that there was a carriage in front of us and a carriage behind us. It seemed kind of unnecessary. I guessed that one or two guards sat on the front bench to guide the horses while the others rested inside.

I was looking around the inside of the carriage for weaknesses. I didn't want to escape yet because I didn't know where we were or if I really was in danger or not. However, my instincts told me I needed to be prepared for anything. I needed more information so I asked, "Where are we going?"

He smiled a full grin and his bright white teeth gleamed back at me. "I am taking you back to the palace to ensure your protection." There were a lot of palaces in the royal Kingdom of Chaos and its four elemental realms. Since he had just said, 'palace' without specifying which one, I assumed he meant his Kingdom's palace, the Palace of Pontus.

"How far of a journey is it?" I asked slightly suspicious. I was a citizen of the Kingdom of Aether, in the Air Realm, but had never left my territory before. Their Kingdom was just south of ours so I figured the trip would take a day and a half, maybe two days.

"Several days. Hopefully, we can get there quickly since we got an early start today," the male replied. I didn't know what he meant by 'several days' because I really didn't think the palace was very far from my home in the Kingdom of Aether. But, then again, I didn't know where the dungeon was that I had been kept in and how far we currently were from my home.

"Where are we now?" I asked. He smiled in response like he knew I was up to something.

"We are at the border, between the Kingdom of Aether and the Kingdom of Pontus," he said like that was good enough. Basically, we could be anywhere along the expansive, mountainous border. I didn't really know how to narrow down the answer anyways. I had never been to the border so any more landmarks would not have helped me orient myself much. At least I knew I was still on the northern tip of the continent, I guessed. If I could escape, I would head north back into the Kingdom of Aether.

We rode for a while in an uncomfortable silence that was interspersed with small talk about the weather, the four kingdoms, and anything else I thought might be useful without being obvious. I would need to get close to him for information. I didn't really have anything better to do anyway. The sun came up shortly after our departure and illuminated the sky. The ground was dusted with a few inches of snow and I could see mountains to one side of us. I needed to get a bearing on where we were.

I was becoming more anxious and angry as the day went on. Even if this was what was best for me, I still should have had a choice. I shouldn't have been dragged out of my home in the dead of night. I didn't respond well to being forced to do things.

We stopped in the early afternoon near a small creek to let the horses get a drink and rest. Once out of the carriage, I noticed that the ground was no longer covered in snow. We must've been traveling south to warmer territories. I could see the ocean off in the distance. I was working up my nerve to demand answers once we got back into the carriage. The male said he was protecting me, and maybe I should trust him, but I wondered why abducting me against my will was necessary. My mind was reeling with ideas of how to get away. I could protect myself from whatever threat he thought I was under. Maybe.

After a quick meal of berries from the nearby trees and bushes, the six remaining armored males retreated back to their carriages. The male and I walked towards the carriage we had been riding in all morning, except it wasn't there. When we got to the general vicinity of it, he offered his hand to help me up the steps. I looked at him confused.

"It's a concealment spell. It will keep us hidden as we travel. For your safety, of course," he said with a slight incline of his head in my direction.

"But, I could see it before," I said, cocking an eyebrow.

"My guard, Jake, placed it on the carriages once we boarded," he said.

I nodded in understanding and placed my hand in his. I stepped a foot forward until it was on the unseen step. I took another step up and leaned into the carriage. The inside was visible. It was quite remarkable magic.

Once seated, I blew out a breath and waited for him to sit down across from me. He sat and looked at me offering me a smile. I finally found the courage to ask my questions.

"What will become of my father, Sire?" I asked, crossing a leg.

"Please, just call me Declan," he said, offering no additional information, smiling.

"Ok, Declan. What will become of my father? Am I to just leave him behind after he is released from his sentence?" I asked a little more bluntly than I intended.

"Your father is not in the danger that you are in, Evelyn. He will remain where he is until he has made penance for his crimes and then he will be released," he said calmly.

"Call me Evie," I said, with a clipped tone because I had already told him that. "Won't he wonder where I am upon his return to our home?" I asked like it was an obvious question.

"You left a note saying that you were traveling to another realm for a few months to visit a friend you previously worked with and haven't seen in a long time," he said casually.

I was shocked. He had covered this up to ensure no one would come to my aid, which was hardly necessary anyway. My father didn't have the resources to find or save me. But I didn't even think that my father would believe the note. He knew I only had one close friend, and she was away at school. My father knew her well and I would've named her in the note, not referred to her as a "friend". Other than that, I didn't make a habit of making friends because I didn't want them. "I don't remember leaving my home. Do you care to elaborate on how I got into your captivity?" I asked, looking him in the eye.

He laughed. "My captivity, Evelyn? Do you not remember the conversations and meetings we have had over the last couple of weeks?" he asked.

My brows furrowed. "Today is the first day we have spoken. I am not sure what you are talking about," but as the words left my mouth, I had this nagging feeling that that was untrue. I started to remember his face, vaguely.

He cocked his head to one side. "I concealed our conversations for your protection. I cast a forgetting spell at the end of each meeting so that you wouldn't let our plan slip to your friends or family, risking exposure," he said like that was no violation of my mind. I was pissed but tried to keep my composure. He added, "We have been preparing to meet on the eve of your twenty-first birthday for the last three weeks. Once the guards came to retrieve you, you panicked and tried to fight them off, but I am not sure why, since you have been in agreement with this plan all along."

"And what plan is that, exactly?" I asked cautiously.

"Evelyn, surely with your power awakened you can shake off a forgetting spell, especially now with the knowledge that one was placed upon you?" he asked with raised brows and a shocked tone. "You are said to be an heir to a Kingdom, making you a duchess. You should be extremely powerful," Declan added, making me feel like I didn't quite measure up.

"Maybe I suffered a head injury when your armored guards dragged me out of my home and threw me in a cell last night," I said with a clipped tone.

"Ok, let's start over. I am Declan, Duke of the Kingdom of Pontus. I've come to help protect you. I will go over our conversations with you. We have plenty of time and need something to talk about anyway," The Duke stated. He shifted forward, resting both of his elbows on his knees. He held his hands out, palms up. We were almost sharing breaths. "Here, place your hands in mine and I will remove the forgetting spells I placed on your mind," he said in a gentle tone.

I leaned forward, slightly suspicious. This whole situation was unsettling, yet I couldn't deny that I was incredibly intrigued. Declan's blue eyes twinkled like he was excited about something.

I slid my hands into his, palms down and warmth washed over me. It was like a fog left my mind and I could remember him clearly. The last several weeks came flooding back to me.

Initially, he had approached me while I was walking home one day from my employer's farm. I assisted a local female in town who traveled from farm to farm to care for sick or injured animals. I worked five days a week from early afternoon to late afternoon. I would often detour through the market and help myself to something for dinner on the way home. I was making my usual pass-through, when Declan bumped into me. I hadn't seen him walking there because I had been watching the owner of an apple stand while I slid an apple into the basket I was carrying. When I looked up at him, he looked down at the apple. He smiled and walked to the owner and handed him some coins. The owner was still in conversation with the next stand owner over. He turned to him and thanked him, then returned back to his conversation. He had never known that Declan was paying for the apple that I was stealing.

He wore more casual clothes and blended into the crowd that day. After he returned from paying the man, he introduced himself, flashing a smile. I remember that he exuded warmth and told me his name was Declan, and he reached out and dropped several coins into my basket. I looked down at the coins and then returned my gaze to his face. He walked with me through the market, casually. I tried to use his coins to pay for things but he always beat me to it. Toward the end of my lap through the market, my basket was full of fruit, vegetables, and bread. And I still had the coins he had given me.

He continued to walk with me, and I let him. We walked by the library, and I went inside with the intention of looking for some reference books on plants and herbs. He followed me in, and we sat at a table and talked, not about anything important. I trusted him during that first meeting due to the kindness he had shown me, and my trust for him had grown more and more each meeting since. When I left the library, we went our separate ways. He headed south and I headed north. I remember thinking about him the whole walk home and how nice it was to be afforded food that day. As I walked home down the dusty street, the realization of my actual lifestyle settled back in. It had never really affected me like that before. The ease of walking through the market and paying for food was distracting and intoxicating.

Father and I had lived in a small town named Ventus. Ventus was impoverished, and we were some of the lower-class citizens. We lived in a small, two-room cottage, with one main room and a small bedroom. The main room should have been where we ate, but there was often no food in the house anyways. I slept on a small bed in the main room that folded up against the wall when I wasn't sleeping and my father occupied the small bedroom. I didn't mind the sleeping arrangements since my bed was closest to the fire. We lived near the Mountains of Boreas on the western edge of the Kingdom of Aether, where it often snowed. I was happy to have a fire nearby while I slept. When father returned that day, he was pleasantly surprised to see all of the food but naturally didn't ask any questions about where it came from or how we could afford it.

Declan and I continued to run into each other at the market. I would leave my employer's farm on the north side of Ventus and travel south toward the market in the center of town. Declan had been buying me food all these weeks. Then we would walk to the small library near my home, before I made my trek back to my cottage alone.

One day, in the library, he came out and told me the truth. He told me he was actually the Duke of the Kingdom of Pontus and that he had visited the market initially because he wanted to escape the attention in his Kingdom and knew no one would recognize him in the Kingdom of Aether at a market. He said that after he ran into me the first day, he kept visiting the market just to see me again. I remembered feeling excited about him being interested in me and even allowing myself to envision a life where I would be taken care of financially.

Upon returning to his Kingdom one day, he had received news that the heir of the Lost Kingdom was being looked for and there were suspicions around it being a low-class citizen living in the Kingdom of Aether, that no one would expect. He knew the heir was almost twenty-one years old and had dark brown hair and turquoise eyes. I fit the description. He said that it was fate that brought us together and he knew he needed to help me return to the Lost Kingdom. He explained that if he didn't help me, other Fae, or who knows what evil would be after me to try and take me for themselves.

I started to remember more and more of our meetings as the memories flooded my mind. I remembered us chatting and walking arm in arm through the market while I snacked on an apple. I could remember us laughing and feeling close to him, like we were old friends. I could even remember the first time we kissed. A memory flashed into my mind of Declan leaning over me as I breathlessly looked up at him while lying on the floor behind a shelf of books in the small library. Books were strewn across the floor, jamming into my skin, while I lay there trying to catch my breath. He was still on his knees, leaning over me, our foreheads touching, with his hands on either side of my head.

I started to remember the many times we had been together. I had feelings of pride knowing I had satisfied him. He had fucked me on the floor of the library regularly. It seemed almost routine. He would slide up my dress and enter me, while we were both still fully clothed. Then he would rock into me until he found his release. When we got up, it was like our little secret. No one would suspect what we had done.

I flashed back to the present time, seeing what I needed to see. I immediately flushed, remembering what had happened between us, and my gaze shot to his. He let out a small laugh, reacting to my blush like he knew what I was remembering too. I slid my hands out of his and sat back while crossing my arms across my chest.

Well, that was going to make this an interesting trip.

Chapter 3

I smiled at Declan, but something pulled at my gut. I started to sort through the memories and piece our conversations together. The Duke, I mean Declan, since we were apparently quite comfortable together, had explained that I was in danger because I was the Lost Duchess of the Kingdom of the Lost.

I had asked Declan some follow-up questions after he restored my memories. How could I have been kidnapped from the Lost Kingdom when no one could return from there? Everyone knew that the Lost Kingdom was surrounded by a magical border that would trap citizens inside. Declan said that I was captured as a small child by King Finlin and Queen Annabell, who had access to enter and exit the Lost Kingdom because they were in charge of the magical border. He said they planned to use me as ransom against the Lord of the Lost Kingdom. Me, the Lost Duchess of the Lost Kingdom. Somehow I was intercepted from the King and Queen of the Kingdom of Chaos. That's where Declan lost me. I knew he could not be implying that my mortal-born father was able to kidnap anything from the King and Queen of Chaos, let alone a lost Duchess.

My father, Thomas Warren, was born to a Fae father and mortal mother. He was of the middle caste, the non-magic born that could study to reclaim their dormant magic genes. My father had a small amount of magic that benefited us very little. He worked a normal mortal job, as a post delivery male, using his magic to enhance his speed on his routes. That way, he could be at the tavern by dinner time. I often met him there in the evenings. It seemed to be the only way we got to spend time together these days.

While I had heard of the Lost Duchess, I thought it was a myth or a legend spread around the Kingdom for entertainment purposes. I found it hard to believe that I could be a long-lost Duchess. Declan said the King and Queen were about to enter the Lost Kingdom again in order to search for me there. They believed I had been returned. Each Kingdom had sent out a search for the Lost Duchess to prevent the King and Queen from embarking on such a dangerous journey. So was Declan saving me or turning me over to the King and Queen?

Declan couldn't quite explain how I wound up with my father, Thomas, but he proposed that maybe some other Fae had kidnapped me and somehow I was intercepted and given to Thomas. He wasn't really sure what happened to the Fae that kidnapped me originally. He just knew more people would come for me now that my magic was revealed to me. I didn't bother to tell him that it wasn't. I didn't want him to have an upper hand on me.

I asked Declan how other Fae would find me. He explained that now that my power was awakened, Fae could seek it and find it. He explained that there were different ways. A spell, "quaerite et invenietis," could help locate objects and other Fae. He said typically only stronger Fae could use the spell. There were also many different magical beings that could reveal information throughout the royal Kingdom of Chaos and had their own unique abilities to track objects. He supposed it would be quite easy to find me, but not while in his protection. He had used protection spells to hide our caravan and keep our location hidden, he said.

I had also asked why the King and Queen would kidnap and use me. They were loved by the entire royal empire, the Kingdom of Chaos, and the four Kingdoms within it. I didn't know much about them and the decisions they made specifically, but

I knew that the consensus was that they were well-liked. Declan couldn't really offer a reason for that. He said that maybe they had made a slip-up or had been blinded by greed in trying to capture me for their own gain. I was skeptical.

Another thing that didn't make sense to me was how I felt towards some of the perceptions I had in the memories he offered me. I didn't voice these to him but I thought about them. The feeling of being taken care of by a male did not line up with my own desires. In the memories Declan showed me, I relished it. I had never been interested in that. In the memories, I was so happy to be financially taken care of while Declan bought everything I wanted in the market but in reality, I didn't care about wealth. In fact, I enjoyed stealing from the market. It was a thrill. In the memories, it almost seemed like we were in a relationship, like he owned me. In reality, I had never been in a relationship nor was I interested. I was not going to be paraded around like some male's property.

I remembered that in the memories, I had felt so proud satisfying Declan sexually. I didn't remember feeling satisfied myself, just the overwhelming sense of wanting to please him. All the visions of us were always with me laying on the floor of the library which wasn't really how I liked to fuck. Some things just left me puzzled. I was pretty strong-willed and my gut was pulling me towards questioning what was going on with my memories.

Declan and I sat facing each other, but I stared out the window of the carriage as I mulled over all of this information. The most pressing issue was my being an heir to a Kingdom that didn't exist. Or, If I even wanted to be a Duchess. Maybe I would be better off returning to my mundane life. I could continue stealing from others in order to fend off starvation and clothe myself so I didn't succumb to frostbite. And I would be fine with it.

Eventually, the carriage came to a slow stop. As the carriage stopped, I jerked backward a little, looking at Declan for an explanation. Declan said, "We are going to camp here for the night. There is a small inn here with three rooms. You and I will share a room." I didn't really know what to think of this sleeping situation. I should probably err on the side of caution.

"I think I should stay in a room of my own," I said hesitantly. Apparently, Declan and I had slept together before. I assumed he would expect it again tonight. My mind was still reeling and I wasn't feeling like myself. I was definitely unable to sort through my feelings for him. However, if his intentions were true and he was truly trying to help me, then maybe I just needed time to accept my memories and the reality of what was going on. Everything had just surprised me and my mind was trying to catch up.

"If we don't share a room, two of the guards will have to sleep outside in one of the carriages. If you and I can stay in one room, then the guards can sleep in the other two rooms while rotating through shifts of guarding our door. Two guards will be outside of our door, guarding it, at all times. It will be safer this way," he said as if it was obvious.

I sighed and relented. He was right. It would be safer and I could always make him sleep on the floor. I didn't want anyone sleeping outside because of me, although it was warmer now than it had been. I grabbed my coat and climbed out of the carriage. Declan handed me a bag that felt like more clothes. After I had climbed out of the carriage, Declan offered me his arm. I looped mine in his and let him pull me along. He smiled at me and I returned the smile. Four guards trailed behind us but I didn't look back to see which ones. Six of us approached the inn, while the other two guards stayed to tend to all the horses.

I flipped my hair to one side with my free hand, running my fingers through it. I was nervous and unsure of myself, which was not typical. I smoothed out my coat. I kind of just wanted to take off running and never look back.

When we walked in, a large being with one eye greeted us. I could tell he was an older cyclops because he was shorter than a typical cyclops would be, only slightly bigger than a Fae in their Fae form. His skin was slightly wrinkled and his one eye had a gray sheen. The large pupil was brown and his thin hair was gray peppered with white.

"Duke Declan!" he exclaimed, warmly. He came around the desk and grabbed a lantern off of a hook on the wall. As he shuffled across the floor, holding a lantern, he led us to the only three rooms he had to offer. I gave Declan a curious glare wondering how he knew there would be rooms available.

He seemed to see the question in my eye and he replied, "I made these arrangements weeks ago." That made sense, I guess, since we had been planning this. I was still trying to wrap my head around the fact that I had known about all of this but had been made to forget.

Declan held out his hand signaling for me to enter the first room on the right. Just past the door, stood the dark-haired guard that I think I had heard him call Jake. He looked at me from the corner of his eye. His gaze was captivating and it was hard to look away. There was something about him I just couldn't quite put my finger on. It nagged at me. He clenched his jaw and, after a brief moment, he looked away again. He stared forward at a blank wall.

I pulled my gaze away from his gorgeous face, turned the handle, and walked into the room. Declan pulled the door closed, remaining in the hallway, and called the guard over to himself to speak in hushed tones. I took this opportunity to pull a nightgown out of my bag and quickly pulled off my clothes. I threw the nightgown over my head while I listened to the exchange coming from the hallways.

"Jake, I want you to oversee the rotations tonight," he said a little more casually than the tone I heard him address the other guards with throughout the day. I was going to start paying more attention to their relationship. I needed to be learning as much as possible in case this situation wasn't what it appeared to be.

After I pulled my nightgown down over my body, I frowned at how it barely covered the bottom of my ass. It was also pulled tight across my chest, leaving gaps between the buttons which revealed my busty frame. I caught a lot of attention from males with my body but was quickly treated differently when I opened my mouth. I spoke how I wanted to, which was probably rougher than most, but I was raised by my single father.

My mother passed away from a bad fever when I was around four. I didn't have many memories of her but in the few I had, she was very caring toward me. She had long, blonde hair and pale skin. She had worked as a school teacher and was an excellent cook. I hadn't had a good meal since she passed away. She and my father loved each other very much and he was devastated by her passing. He just seemed lost to the grief ever since. The grief seemed to get worse over time instead of better. I tried to cut my father some slack for his drinking after suffering such a loss, but I had lost her too and seventeen years had passed now.

My father and I were close, nonetheless. When he wasn't imprisoned, I would visit the tavern to see him. I would head home earlier than he would, but eventually, he would stumble in. He always pulled my blanket up and kissed my cheek before heading to bed. He was delicate with me, even though he put the tavern and his ale before me. Occasionally, he would skip the tavern and we would spend the evening talking and drinking at home. But that was a rare treat, sadly.

My nights at the tavern were rough. Males didn't know how to act after they had a few drinks in them. I learned how to fight and defend myself at a young age. My father took pride in how well I fought, drank, and played darts and cards. I was excellent at darts and was recently able to outdrink most males there.

Declan knocked before slowly opening the door, interrupting my thoughts. He didn't wait for a response before he started to walk into the room. After entering the room, he started slowly slipping out of his coat. It was a sturdy black material with the crest of the Kingdom of Pontus. There were gold and blue embellishments around the cuffs and buttons. It was lacking in military flourishes, though, and I wondered if Declan either hadn't served or was very young.

Underneath, he wore a long-sleeved white button-up shirt. He started to unbutton the sleeves at his wrist and then worked on unbuttoning the buttons down the front. He reached the bottom button and pulled the shirt open with both hands. He slipped out of the shirt and put it on a chair with his coat.

He looked at me and found that I had been watching his every movement. I had been studying his body. He looked me up and down and his gaze heated as it raked over my body.

Feeling exposed, I blurted, "I didn't have anything in the bag that fit." I shrugged my shoulders, and his eyes flared. Maybe I should've just kept my other clothes on.

Slowly Declan said, "I think it fits fine. Perfect, even." He had a mischievous look in his eye but blinked it away and fixed his features to look impassive. His lashes were long and blonde like his hair. He had blueish gray eyes and was very handsome. I wondered about his age after seeing his coat.

"How old are you?" I asked, not able to wonder anymore. I didn't know much about him except that he was the Duke of the Kingdom of Pontus. I could make assumptions about him, of course. He would most likely have the elemental affinity of water, and his form should be a water creature, perhaps a merman or a selkie.

"Twenty-seven," he said, flatly. If he was that old, I wondered why he didn't have any military accolades, but I thought it was stupid to get held up on. If he was a Duke, it wasn't out of the realm of possibilities. He would be quite wealthy. Maybe he had multiple coats.

Declan had a fairly nice body. He was muscular - slightly above average. It was certainly better than some of the males back home that I had been with. It wasn't that I slept around, but I had been with my fair share of gentlemen. It was improper for a lady, but I didn't care. I wanted to explore and find what I liked. I hadn't found it yet, that was for sure. The males back home didn't seem to know what they were doing. My first time was with a boy from school. It had been a total disaster. We were both sixteen and had snuck off into the woods behind his house. Laying in the leaves, I had gotten bitten by fire ants, and he could never find his release. From between my legs, he looked nervous. We both left disappointed. I guess things had improved since then, at least. I slept with long-term acquaintances, typically. All were just casual encounters that were convenient. I had never been in a relationship, and it was the last thing I was interested in.

A few tense moments passed, but neither of us moved. I felt a warmth wash over me, and I forgot all of my cares and concerns. I suddenly acknowledged that there was an amazing male that standing before me. With our gazes locked on each other, I bit my bottom lip, unable to stop myself. Declan's eyes widened slightly a little before a smile broke out on his face. Declan stood there confidently. Confidence turned me on. He cleared his throat, "Uhm, which side of the bed would you like?"

He gestured to the bed, and I walked around to climb in. I pulled the sheets down and sat, peeking over my shoulder at him.

"We will have to get a pretty early start tomorrow. I am happy with the progress we made today. I think we will get to our destination in a few days," Declan said as he started unbuttoning his pants.

I considered how far the palace was and wondered how long the trip would be from where I had been living in the Kingdom of Aether. I now assumed we were traveling to the Palace of the Kingdom of the Lost. We would be traveling from one point of the kingdom to another. I expected it to take at least a week, but Declan seemed to think it would only take a few days.

"Is there not a quicker way to travel by using magic?" I asked. I really didn't know, but I couldn't understand why a Duke would travel like a non-magic citizen born into the bottom caste.

"There are a few reasons why we can't travel magically. Firstly, I have us coated in protection spells that don't hold when we travel by magic. Secondly, traveling by magic can throw off alarms, causing us to be detected by the King," he said.

"What kind of alarms?" I asked.

"There may be protection spells on you, and we aren't sure. If we start using a bunch of magic to travel, it will notify the Fae who cast the spell," he said.

"Wouldn't that have been my parents?" I asked, like it was an obvious question.

"Or your kidnapper, we don't know. I've been ordered to deliver you without the use of magic," he said, shrugging.

I looked over my shoulder again to see if Declan had crawled into the bed. I caught a glimpse of him releasing his pants, and they fell to the floor. I swallowed hard. I looked away quickly and slid into bed, laying on my back and staring at the ceiling. I thought of my best friend, Jude, and how I wished she was on this journey with me. Would I ever see her again?

Trying to distract myself with other thoughts wasn't working.

I heard Declan step out of his pants and kick them aside as I continued to stare at the ceiling, refusing to look at him. I had this overwhelming attraction to him that hadn't been there a few moments ago. He walked over to the lantern on the wall and blew out the flame. Then he approached the bed.

After pulling back the sheets, he bent and sat on the edge of the bed. He picked one leg up and swung it up onto the bed while the other leg followed, slipping into the sheets. Was he climbing into the bed naked? Had he not put any night clothes on?

Trying to distract myself, I said, "Declan, when will my elemental affinities reveal themselves to me?" I didn't want him to know my weaknesses and the fact that I hadn't received my elements, but I needed to know and didn't have anyone else to ask at the moment.

"You received them at midnight last night, so you should try to see what natural elements listen to you. Happy Birthday, by the way," he said. "Do you not feel anything?" he asked. Easier said than done.

"I feel like my blood is moving swiftly through my veins but it has been that way for a while now. I am not sure how to activate my power or how to use it," I said. I really wished I had taken this more seriously in school. I had always anticipated that if and when my elemental affinities would surface, I would run to my best friend Jude's house and she would tell me everything I needed to know. I never expected to find myself in this situation.

"It's easy; you just will it. Think of it as dominating nature and taking what you want from it," he said, rolling over to face me. "Try it, cast a light," he said. Nothing said I would be able to harness light.

I tried to think of anything but lying here next to this naked male. I had found myself in quite a situation. I wondered what would happen between us tonight.

"Focus," he said bluntly, but I could almost hear his smile. It was like he could feel my lust.

I took a deep breath in and slowly released it. After a few moments, I said, "I'm sorry." I just couldn't will the fire to my fingers.

"Maybe tomorrow, if we have some time, we can practice. You'll also have to try and sort out what form you can shift into. That can take some time to activate, and not everyone can shift at first," Declan said casually. It sort of seemed like he was happy to help me with this uncharted path, like we were quickly becoming friends. Or had been friends, I guessed, remembering the memories he had shown me.

I couldn't reconcile my feelings. I was skeptical about what he had revealed to me in the memories, and not everything seemed right. But he had also shown me kindness in the market. He could've easily just kept walking. He was also trying to save me from the dangers awaiting me. But in this moment, I wanted him. Feeling closer to Declan than I should, I asked, "have you always wanted to be a royal? You will eventually become the Lord of Pontus. Is that what you want?"

He thought about it, his face frowning in concentration. After a few moments of silence, he responded, "I haven't always wanted to rule. I have seen some good rulers and some bad rulers. I have a good sense of who I want to be as a Lord and what I can do for my kingdom. I think I will be ready to rule when fate chooses. My parents still have many good years, and I have a lot to learn from them," he finished thoughtfully. That was a sweet answer.

Declan reached out to take my hand. He wrapped his large hand around mine, and I didn't pull away. I felt torn until he made contact. He rubbed the back of my hand with a light touch and warmth spread throughout my body. After several long moments, I felt fatigue taking over. I felt so relaxed in his company. All of my previous thoughts had faded away. I couldn't even remember what I was worried about before. How could I not worship this male? He was perfect in every way.

He pulled my hand up to his mouth and lightly kissed the back of it. He set my hand back down and slowly ran his hand up my arm to my shoulder, sending a shiver down my spine. I placed my hand back on my hip as I faced him and goosebumps covered my arms at the softness of his touch. He ran his hand up and down my arm slowly a few more times. As he reached my fingertips on the last pass, he didn't stop and return to my shoulder as he had done previously. His hand kept moving down my side and across my hip.

He ran his hand over the swell of my ass, cupping it and pulling me towards him until our bodies crashed into each other. I lifted my leg over him as our mouths met to confirm that this was what I wanted, too. He kissed me quickly, coming back for more and more. His tongue slid into my mouth, as things heated up between us.

He was kissing me with an urgency, and he shifted me onto my back and positioned himself in between my legs, gripping the back of my arms to pull me up into a sitting position. Once I was sitting, he pulled my nightgown up over my head in one swift motion. My long, brown hair fell down my back to my waist. He was, in fact, completely naked, like he had known this was going to happen.

I was overcome with emotions, mainly lust. As soon as my hands were free of my nightgown, I held onto Declan's shoulders as we began moving. I clawed at his back, gripping him, as he pulled me to the edge of the bed. We kissed each other fiercely, and I felt desire thrumming through my body. I wanted him everywhere. I wanted him to touch me all over my body.

He tried to lay me on my back, but I slid off the bed and stood before him. I never surrendered to a male, especially during sex.

I was ready and I needed more of him. I dropped to my knees before Declan as he stood. He reached behind me, grabbing the back of my head and pulling me towards him.

I took his length in my mouth as he tipped his head back and let out a moan of pleasure. I started working my mouth up and down. Continuing the up and down motion, I peered up to look at him meeting his eyes. He uttered a wild noise, like a growl. Behind him, I noticed tendrils of bright red dust escaping him. I assumed it was his natural aura but was confused about it being red. Why would he emit red if he was from the Kingdom of Pontus? His natural aura should've been blue, right? He wasn't using the fire element so I wasn't sure why red was escaping him.

He quickly pulled me to a standing position by my elbows as I considered it, breaking me from my thoughts. He guided me backward until my knees hit the bed, and I sat on the edge. He pushed my shoulders, urging me to lay down. He stood before me, and I knew what was coming next. The anticipation excited me. I was waiting for him to kneel before me. But he didn't. He climbed up on the bed, on top of me, and entered me. I tried to lean up to kiss him but he leaned over and started to suck on my neck instead. He started rocking back and forth, but he didn't fill me. He continued moving weakly.

"Do you like that, Evie?" he said so seductively. I focused on my breathing, unable to answer him. I clutched the sheets with both hands at my sides as he began pounding into me sloppily. No, I didn't like it. I could barely feel it, actually.

He sped up until he found his release, letting out a moan as he shuddered. Surely that wasn't it? It had been so quick. He exhaled, smiling, and then he rolled off of me. I lay there staring up at the ceiling for a moment. I slid back into the position I had been when we initially laid down until my head was on the pillow to allow for him to get into the bed too. I was still looking up at the ceiling. I should tell him how I felt about this. Was he really not going to satisfy me? I rolled over to speak to him and found him asleep. I was shocked. He was already breathing deeply, not caring that he had left me wanting. Surely, he hadn't missed my boredom or my lack of release.

I was left feeling extremely confused. That was one of the worst sexual encounters I had ever had. Declan didn't even leave me satisfied. He didn't even try.

Chapter 4

We awoke the following day and dressed quickly to set off on a full day's journey. I watched Declan get ready as if he forgot I was there. Ready to go, he headed to the door and stopped. He crossed the room back to where I was standing and put his hands on my arms.

"Thanks for last night," he said, smiling.

"I was actually hoping we could talk about that," I replied. I hadn't really figured out how to nicely question his terrible performance.

"Of course, we have all day to talk about it. And maybe do it again," he said with a smile and walked towards the door and exited. I had a frustrated look on my face, but I followed him out the door, rolling my eyes.

As we walked out of our room, the guards were smiling, all but Jake. It dawned on me that they probably heard everything. I hadn't made any audible noises, since I had barely been involved, but Declan had. I could feel my cheeks and neck reddening but I kept my head held high and walked outside to the carriages. The expression on Jake's face was hard to read as I walked past him.

They must've thought we had had an amazing night together but we hadn't. Or, at least, I hadn't. Declan had gotten up and dressed so quickly without saying a word to me. He had a smile on his face though. He had to notice that I was behaving differently. I wasn't being warm towards him, but then again we really didn't know each other at all. He couldn't have possibly known what to expect from me.

He walked outside to find the carriages awaiting us and I followed. They were not concealed yet, so we could easily board them. Declan held out his hand to help me in. I wanted to push it away but didn't to avoid causing a scene. Once I was inside, he hurried in after me and pulled me to sit down beside him instead of across from him. I let out a surprised laugh. Maybe he was going to try to cheer me up about last night. Maybe it was a fluke and he had just been tired. I had hope.

We embarked on our long journey. I laid my head on Declan's shoulder as he interlaced our fingers. I noticed his power ring for the first time. Every Fae with awakened power had one. We were to retrieve it from the Oracle around our twenty-first birthday, something I should currently be doing.

A power ring was custom-made for each Fae. The Oracle was a magical being that created it in the Fae's presence once they found her. From what I had been told, the hunt for the Oracle was a task in and of itself. Declan's middle stone was black and he had two small stones on the outside that were yellow and green. I had always heard a Fae's citizenship and elements were encompassed in their power ring which meant Declan's center stone should be blue since he was the Duke of the Kingdom of Pontus. I assumed, from the ring that the green was for earth and the yellow was for light. I was confused about the black center stone. And since he was the Duke of the Kingdom of Pontus there should be some blue somewhere for water. I must just be tired and confused. The lack of sleep last night and the swaying of the carriage lulled me into a deep sleep.

I awoke, some unknown amount of time later, as the carriage slowed to a stop. I rubbed my eye with the back of my hand, thinking back to my injuries. I had tried to remember the words Declan had used to heal me in case I needed them someday. But they weren't words I recognized. I should ask him to tell me again. That spell would surely come in handy in the future.

I stretched my arms and sat up, leaning away from Declan. I turned towards him and smiled, but he didn't return it. Declan was acting way different than yesterday. He wasn't chatting or interested anymore. Maybe he was just tired. Or, perhaps, he had gotten what he wanted and was no longer attempting to win me over. My brows furrowed and pain pulled at my gut.

"We're going to stop here and rest before we travel some more," he said. He moved to exit the carriage without any more explanation. I climbed out of the carriage after him and immediately saw Jake. He turned to look at me, with his captivating eyes, and watched me walk out of the carriage with Declan. I could feel his eyes burning into the back of my head as we passed. Should I be worried?

We walked near a stream, and Declan caught me by the arm to stop me. "Try to draw water away from the stream, Evelyn. You should be able to manipulate it if you have the elemental affinity to harness water," he said.

I held my palms up, not really sure where to start. I closed my eyes thinking of something I wanted the water to do. I should focus on something easy.

"Don't overthink it. Just try to force it to do what you want it to do," he said, from behind me.

I inhaled and let out a slow breath. With my palms outstretched, I tried to force the water to rise. Rise from the earth, I commanded the stream in my head. I popped my eyes open to find it unchanged. It continued to flow in its current path as if mocking me. After a few attempts, I gave up and turned back to face Declan.

He smiled and shrugged, "We can keep trying at our next stop. There is no rush. You are safe and protected here with my royal guards and me," he said. This was more talking than he had done all day. I felt reassured that I was just overthinking things and that things were actually fine between us. He reached out and pinched my chin, and smiled. He threw an arm over my shoulder and started guiding me back to the carriage.

I thought about what he said and I figured that that was true. I didn't need to rush my abilities. It would come to me in due time and I needed to be patient. I was surrounded by armed guards that could harness their elements. I just didn't like relying on others, typically. But what the hell else was I going to do?

I nodded and smiled. I turned to walk back to the area the carriage had been. From a distance, I could see Jake looking at me. He stood tall and broad. His jet-black hair blew slightly in the breeze. He had chiseled features and a firm chest. As soon as I noticed him looking at me, he turned away from me.

I should say something to Declan but I wasn't sure what. Maybe that was just Jake's job. He was hired to watch me and protect me, so he would have to look at me. It just felt different. It felt intense.

We walked back over to the vicinity of the carriage. It was nice to get out of the carriage and walk a bit. I wasn't used to sitting so much. In my spare time, I liked to explore the woods near my house. I climbed trees and would watch animals on the forest floor. Occasionally, some creature would chase me and I loved the rush of adrenaline. One time, a boar chased me into a cave and the cave ended. I had picked up a rock and knocked it in the head and fled. I always carried a rock with me after that experience. I enjoyed chasing animals and laying traps. I just liked to run wild and free.

When we approached the carriage, Declan took me by the hand to guide me to it. He seemed to be able to locate it better than I could. He offered his hand to help me in. I took it, seeing it as an effort on his part. We climbed back into the carriage, sitting next to each other again. The carriage lurched forward as we began to travel. I was seated next to Declan, trying not to focus on how confused I felt. He didn't seem to waste any thought on it.

As the carriage started to roll again, he looked at me. I really wanted everything to be ok between us. I was torn between saying something about last night or not. Maybe I should tell him I sought pleasure too. But wasn't that obvious? He gave me a quick kiss on the cheek.

I turned to face him and he reached his arm across me and up into my hair. He pulled me in for a kiss on the lips, then another. After a few quick kisses, I noticed his other hand traveling down to unfasten his pants. He reached over and took my hand and placed it where his pants were now open, revealing himself to me.

It was too late to speak up about last night and I felt the overwhelming need to pleasure him. I found pleasure in it myself, forgetting my own release. I started working him up and down with my hand and he moaned in my mouth. I liked the power I held over males with my body and sexuality.

I slid to the floor and knelt before Declan. I looked at him from under my hooded eyes, as I took the length of him in my mouth. He slid his fingers into my hair, bracing the back of my head, encouraging me up and down. I began working him nice and slow in and out of my mouth. I wanted to get him ready and then I would slide into his lap to join him. After a few passes up and down, I reached down to slide my pants down my waist. As I shifted to push myself up, he exploded in my mouth with a moan. I swallowed once, then twice, then a third time knowing that my chance for release was over. What the fuck?

Before he noticed, I slid my pants back up my waist. I climbed back up onto the seat next to him and he patted me on the knee. Then he leaned his head back and closed his eyes, with his pants still open. I turned and stared out the window. I wasn't really sure what to say to him or how to fix this. I didn't even really know what I expected out of this exchange.

Declan and I didn't speak much for the rest of the trip. As the sun lowered in the sky, the carriage began to slow.

"We will be creating our own shelter tonight. We will all stay together in a cave," Declan said. "You can remain here until I come back for you when the arrangements are ready," Declan said, exiting the carriage.

I figured this meant that we would not be repeating last night's activities, which may be a relief. I looked down at my hands and wondered what life would be like where I was going. I was having a hard time understanding where I stood with Declan and how I felt about him. I bounced between an overwhelming sense of wanting to sleep with him and being annoyed with him. I was still having a hard time believing I was a lost child to someone of wealth and status, which was actually the more important issue here.

My father had loved me like I was his child and we lived our whole lives together. Would he really keep this secret from me? Could it be possible that he hadn't known? The whole thing just didn't make sense yet. Maybe I needed to travel to see him to discuss this with him.

I decided to climb out of the carriage and watch Declan cast his earth magic. Maybe I needed to see magic demonstrated in order to learn to use my own. I opened the carriage door and standing within an arm's distance of my face was Jake. His eyes widened in surprise like he wasn't expecting me to pop out. I was surprised to have come so close to him too. I paused there, staring at him for a moment. I saw him swallow.

"Do you need something?" he asked, softly. He spoke a lot more kindly to me than I expected. He looked away from me and I turned to see what he was looking at. Declan was approaching and he didn't look happy. Then Jake and I looked at eachother again. My pulse sped up.

"No," I said, not understanding what was going on between us. I climbed down the steps and brushed past him. Our arms barely made contact and a spark snapped between us. I grabbed my arm and looked at him, searching his face for answers.

He looked at me, emotionless. I couldn't read anything about him. Just then, Declan approached me.

"I thought you were going to wait for me inside," he said, clipped. It was like he didn't want me out here. Maybe he was just worried I would be exposed.

"I thought I would come out and watch you create the cave," I said. He thought for a moment like he was trying to reel in his emotions. I hadn't done anything wrong and I didn't see what the big deal was so I didn't understand his response.

"Ok," he said slowly and with a shrug. Taking my hand, he led me away to the side of a hill. He pulled me along like a child. He held up his palms and green earth magic shot out in a blast.

A cave was immediately carved into the hillside. It was large with only one entrance and I could see the back of it. It was made of dark gray stone and was just tall enough for all of us to walk into it with space above our heads. I would be sleeping in one large room with seven males, that was a new one for me. The ride had made me tired and I hoped I would get to sleep quickly. It wasn't going to be comfortable and I was concerned about what creatures may be roaming out here in the woods.

"You may enter," he said. I remained where I was, looking around. I noticed that the guards were absent. "The guards are checking to make sure the area is safe," Declan said to me.

Off to one side, a werewolf emerged from the woods. The large, brown wolf quickly changed back into his Fae form and I recognized him as one of Declan's guards shortly after I had jumped in surprise. I had thought we were being attacked for a moment.

A large bull like creature, a Minotaur I presumed, came bounding out of the woods from another direction. He shifted back into another one of Declan's guards then walked in the direction of the cave.

A centaur came running in from the woods, changing forms mid-run. The half man, half horse shrunk back to his normal Fae size. Next to him, Jake emerged from the woods and sped up to us, leaving a blur in his wake. He must be of the vampire form with increased speed and agility.

Jake walked past us and entered the cave too. Everyone was heading in that direction so I moved forward too. Jake held up his palms, calling on the elements. Using earth magic, he began lining the floor with soft, fluffy moss and grass to make it more comfortable to sleep on. Everyone moved to spread out to lay down to sleep so I followed. I walked over to the left side looking over my shoulder supposing Declan would follow me. I was shocked and hurt when Declan headed for the other side of the cave. I sat down and looked around with a feeling of confusion. Declan made me feel unsure of myself and my place in his presence with others. Yet when it was just us, something changed and I couldn't quite understand it. When we were alone I felt strongly towards him. Could he control my emotions towards him somehow? I hadn't considered that before.

I looked up, taking in the structure. The cave was one large room made of rock and looked natural. The moss and grass that Jake had willed onto the ground was a nice touch. The guards were all laying down now, some of them were even snoring like this was no big deal. I hugged my knees and rested my head on my arms. After a moment, I looked over my shoulder to see that it was Jake who laid closest to me.

Jake lay on his back with his arms up under his head. His eyes were closed but I wasn't sure if he was asleep or not. He laid there, still wearing the pants and boots he had been wearing earlier. He had taken off his coat and was left in a long-sleeved black shirt.

His eyes slowly opened, to find me staring at him. We made eye contact and I turned away quickly. I laid down on my side, facing the cave entrance. I closed my eyes, but could hear noises coming from outside of the cave that I didn't recognize. I could hear howling and grumbling off in the distance. Behind me I could hear Jake start to move. He stood and walked into my view of the cave opening. I could see his build now that his coat was off. He had an incredibly muscular frame. He didn't look too worried about the noises that were plaguing me. He held up his hands with his outstretched palms. He whispered something I didn't recognize, and the cave opening was covered with a soft lilac glow.

He must've used some type of protection spell to cover the cave. I almost asked what he had done, but I didn't know if he would tell me. Had he done that just to calm my fears? I also had to wonder why Declan hadn't cast the protection spell on the cave entrance since he was so worried about someone intercepting me. He had just seemed ready to sleep when we got here.

"I cast a protection spell over the cave. You are safe here and you should get some sleep," Jake said to me as he passed me on his way back to his portion of the cave floor. When he had come back from casting the protection spell, I noticed that he sat a little closer to me than he had been. It should've been Declan reassuring me but he was already fast asleep, not caring if I was ok or not. I looked at Jake as he spoke. He really was the most attractive male I had ever seen. He had bright green eyes, visible to me in the glow of the cave mouth, that were captivating to look at. He broke our eye contact and looked in Declan's general direction. I turned and faced forward again. I blew out a breath I didn't realize I had been holding.

I lay back down and closed my eyes again. I heard Jake shift into a laying position again too. I needed to rest and prepare for another long day's journey. I tried to push my confusing feelings for Declan and my intrigue over Jake out of my mind. Maybe with a good night's sleep, I could harness my elemental affinities tomorrow. I needed to focus on that. Eventually, I slipped into a restless sleep.

Chapter 5

The next morning, we awoke to a cloudy overcast sky. The protection spell had been removed and several of the guards had already exited the cave. I shifted to a sitting position and rubbed my eyes. I saw Declan outside the cave so I got up. I walked out of the cave to meet him where he was seated on a log by a small fire. I offered him a smile and he gave me a half-smile in return. He patted the log next to him gesturing me to sit. I sat next to him and he held out a handful of berries. I cupped my hands to accept them and he dropped them into my hands. On a rock next to him was a charred dead squirrel. "I cooked some meat too if you want any," he said, picking up the squirrel which was skewered on a stick.

"No, I am fine. Thanks," I added, revolted. I looked around at the clearing and saw the guards returning from the woods again. The werewolf guard had blood on his mouth and realization dawned on me. They must all be out hunting for their desired meals.

A griffon landed hastily in front of us. It flapped its wings backwards trying to slow itself down. The flapping was raising dust from the ground and throwing my hair all around my face. Once its feet had a firm hold on the ground, it shifted back into a guard. He was now holding a fish in his hand. "I brought one back for you, Declan," he said.

"Could you have landed a little further away, Gareth? You covered me in dust," Declan said, infuriated. He gestured to the dust on his shoes. I assumed he had a point but this male had been considerate enough to bring him a fish. He should've thanked him.

Declan set down his squirrel and snatched the fish. He skewed it on a stick and held it over the fire as he raised the squirrel to his mouth and took a bite out of it. I thought to myself that I hadn't seen Declan shift into any form. I wondered what his form was.

"What form can you shift into Declan?" I asked, casually. It should be some type of water creature but I guessed we hadn't been near any water, so he hadn't needed to shift. He looked at me but continued to chew. Then, he ripped off another piece of meat and chewed on it. Another guard approached and started speaking with Declan and he never returned to my question. Weird.

Once everyone was satiated, we boarded the carriages to travel again. I sat next to Declan in the carriage, just like the previous day, even though I was pretty annoyed with him. He seemed cold towards me and slightly bored. Maybe he had lost interest now. Or maybe he was just moody. I had decided I wouldn't pleasure him again until we talked. I just wasn't really sure what a good lead-in to that conversation was.

Suddenly, the carriage jolted. It felt as though something heavy had landed on top. I jumped and my head whipped around to Declan. He had wide eyes and looked scared. He was frozen.

"What the fuck was that?" I asked.

"I don't know," Declan said, looking scared.

"Declan, we need to exit the carriage and see what's going on," I said.

"No," he said shortly. "The guards will deal with it," he added. I was shocked. I couldn't imagine sitting around and letting someone fight my battles for me. I went to stand to exit the carriage, and he pushed me back down into my seat. "Sit down, Evelyn. What are you doing?" he spat.

I heard several voices outside the carriage, and I pushed the curtain aside to peek out the window. Three guards stood with their backs to the carriage, looking in all directions around us.

Suddenly, three large animals I had never seen before, jumped out of the woods. All three of them were black with fur on their back. Their chests and underbellies were covered in scales. They had large, green eyes with black slits in the centers. Spikes lined their face and trailed down their backs. They crawled on all fours and had long tails with a collection of spikes on the end. They looked like they had crawled right out of someone's nightmares.

Jake shot around the carriage and sliced the one farthest to the right up under its neck with a sword. The three guards didn't move to help him. With Jake's increased speed, he shot to the next one and decapitated it completely. He moved towards the third and it snapped at him. He jumped back and then thrust the sword into its underbelly. All three black beasts were pouring black blood onto the ground. He withdrew his sword from the animal's stomach and turned to look back in the direction from where it came.

I turned to look at Declan who remained frozen in place. He looked terrified and was acting like a scared child. What the fuck was wrong with him? I turned back to face the window. I heard a scream coming from the other side of the carriage. I knew Declan wouldn't let me approach the window on that side for fear of me attempting to exit the carriage to fight, so I just continued to watch outside of my window.

A ball of orange light shot directly at Jake from the trees beyond us. He batted it down easily with a flash of his own magic. Then, several blasts of multiple colors of magic shot out at the guards. There were balls of yellow, orange, red, and even black shooting at them from multiple directions. Jake threw up a shield which appeared to be a sheet of white in front of himself and the three guards with him. He truly was a skilled leader.

"Evelyn, do not worry. You are in good hands," Declan said. I turned to face him with pinched brows. I think he said it more for himself than for me. I was disgusted by a male that sat back and let others fight their battles for them. Many things about Declan annoyed me but this was the worst. Jake could die out there.

Several males, maybe ten, broke out through the woods. They all wore black armor and I couldn't identify what Kingdom they fought for, if any. They all had a sword in one hand and an outstretched palm in the other.

Jake swung a sword upward and decapitated the first male. Multiple males attacked the guards and they all broke into sword fights. Swords were clanging and dirt was flying. I was unable to take my eyes off of Jake though. He fought with the ease of a trained fighter.

The whole carriage jolted and I shuddered. I looked up and could see through slats in the wood. There was a large beast on top of the carriage scratching at the wood and rocking it from side to side. I clutched onto the wall of the carriage to keep from falling. I suddenly felt like I was in a cage, like a trapped animal. One of the guards appeared on top of the carriage and lifted the beast up into the air, showing incredible strength. There was a snap and the beast went limp. The guard pushed the beast off the side of the carriage and the whole carriage rocked under the shift in weight. I looked out the window again and saw a large brown, hairy beast in a heap on the ground. The guard jumped down from the roof of the carriage and landed on the ground next to the beast. It was Jake. He searched the area then looked at the guards nearest to him. One was panting but unharmed. The second was sitting on the ground with his arms resting on his knees. The third was clutching his side, blood running down. Jake moved over to him quickly and rested his hand on his shoulder. Jake's mouth was moving but I couldn't possibly hear him. The male's side started glowing green and he removed his hand standing more upright. He looked at his side then to Jake. They had an exchange and the guard looked grateful. Jake clapped him on the back, then scanned the area again before disappearing to walk around the front of the carriage.

There was a knock on the door and Declan leaned up to push it open. Jake stood there dirty and sweaty, hands in his pockets. He looked rough and rugged, and I actually felt my breathing hitch. He was captivating. I finally remembered to blink. He looked at me first before cutting his eyes to Declan. The mere second we made eye contact made my stomach flutter.

"We are going to go scan the area. We will be back in a few moments," Jake said to Declan.

"Ok, Jake, whatever you advise," Declan said. He didn't really sound in charge. Jake nodded and turned to leave. Declan sat back down and slung his arm around my back. He gave me a squeeze and then returned his arm to his lap.

"Who do you suppose attacked us, Declan?" I asked.

"Probably someone trying to intercept you, Evelyn. I remained in the carriage to protect you," he added. I wasn't convinced, but I guess that would make sense. Except he had seemed so scared. We waited a few long moments. I peeked out the window and the guards were all gone. I assumed they were off in the woods.

I turned back to face Declan. "How did they see the carriage?" I asked, wondering aloud.

"They must've heard us. I don't know how they got close enough to our location though," he said. Sometimes he was talkative and answered my questions and sometimes he didn't. It was strange but I was glad he was answering them now. Declan put his hand over on my knee and started running his hands up and down my thigh when there was a knock at the door.

"Come in," Declan yelled.

Jake opened the door and looked at me first again. His gaze went from my eyes to Declan's hand on my knee. He then looked to Declan with an emotionless expression. "It's all clear," Jake said.

"How many were there?" Declan asked.

"Forty five," Jake answered, matter-of-factly.

I looked to Declan and his eyebrows raised. I had my arms crossed as Declan's hand started to travel up my leg again. I looked at his hand then to Jake. Mine and Jake's gaze met but Declan didn't notice. He had laid his head back and closed his eyes. Jake's eyes darted down to my crossed arms then back to my eyes. I saw a hint of a smile on Jake's face as he shut the door. I wondered what that was about.

After a few moments, the carriage started rolling forward again. I laid my head back too. I must've dozed off again with my head on Declan's shoulder. I awoke suddenly as the carriage jolted downward. It felt like the carriage was moving differently. It didn't seem to roll over rough terrain anymore. In fact, it felt like it was being pulled through sand or dirt.

I lifted my head from Declan's shoulder and peeked out the curtained window in the side of the carriage. It looked like we were traveling across a sandy beach. I turned to face him, confused and noticed that his face looked cold and emotionless.

We slowed to a stop. "What route is this?" I asked. He did not answer, back to his bad fucking moods. Instead, he got up and stepped out of the carriage. I peeked out the door and saw all of the guards approaching Declan like they were having a meeting. I slid out of the carriage, assuming it was safe to go out.

I walked down the steps leading out of the carriage and took in my surroundings. As I turned back, I could see that the carriage was still concealed and could see clear through it to the sandy shore on the other side. We were on a rocky beach lined with large caves. I walked up the beach, taking in the new sites. I recognized the Caves of Echidna from books I read as a child.

The Caves, named after the goddess of Monsters, Echidna, were said to be full of the worst type of Fae that had gone mad or had been born monsters. It was a prison of sorts where the monsters ruled themselves. Spells bound its residents to the Caves so that they could never escape. It was almost like they locked them in and threw away the key. I wasn't sure what we were doing here. I got lost taking in my surroundings and several moments passed. I turned to look for Declan as he walked back to the area the carriage was in.

I called out to him, "Why did we stop here?" I started to get nervous as realization dawned on me. Declan held up his hand, freezing me in place. I looked at him confused.

"You're staying here, Duchess," he almost spat. His face was completely void of emotions.

"I am staying here? At the Caves of Echidna?" With every word, my voice got higher pitched as panic built in my chest.

"Yes, I am leaving you here where you belong. I will return for you when it is time to claim my bounty," he spat.

"Declan, I don't understand...." I said in horror. I looked at the guards as they started to approach their respective carriages. Jake looked over his shoulder at me with what looked like panic in his eyes. His hair was gently blowing in the ocean breeze as his gaze flicked from mine to Declan's. I was still frozen in place but I began to plead again, "Declan, please just-"

"You're staying here, Evelyn. What is so hard to understand about that?" Declan interrupted. A smile broke across his face. He looked crazy.

"What has been going on between us then?" I questioned. Most of the guards were approaching the carriages so I knew no one could hear us.

"I am a Siren, Evelyn. I feed off of emotions. It fuels my power. I fed off of your lust. It was also... fun? I think that's the word." He shrugged and walked up the steps to the concealed carriage. My mouth dropped open. He continued, "I will return to get you when they're ready for you." He sounded so proud of himself. My whole body heated, as my emotions built, even though the breeze was strong enough to blow my hair back.

I began to plead, "Declan, please don't put me in the caves-"

"Bye, Evelyn," he interrupted as he opened the door to the carriage, exposing the visible inside, and climbed in. I was still frozen in place but panic was rising inside me. Before he shut the door of the carriage, he raised his palm up to me. Suddenly, I felt an overwhelming force pushing me to the cave entrance. My body started to move on its own accord as I was carried toward the dark cave mouth. When he shut the door, the carriage disappeared completely.

An internal battle broke out within me. I was mentally warring with myself, trying to get my body to listen. I was getting closer and closer to confinement in the caves. My body was moving but I didn't want to go. My feet were sliding through the sand leaving a trail behind me. I finally reached the rocky ground at the mouth of the caves.

As I was forced by the invisible hand closer to the cave entrance, I looked inside and saw that there was a steep drop. I couldn't see the bottom because it was dark. I started to hear crying and growling coming from inside the cave, making my blood feel like ice running through my veins. I felt a sudden pop as if the spell had broken and the full weight of my body returned to me as I regained control over myself. Had I somehow broken the spell through sheer will?

I stood on the rocks near the cave mouth. I was alone but unbound. Judging by the distant sounds, the carriages had already pulled away. I didn't want to return with them anyways. I needed to get out of here quickly in case they realized that the spell that was supposed to force me into the caves had been broken. The whole beach was lined with caves and I was beginning to hear shrieks from the depths of the dark cave nearest to me. I was completely exposed on the beach. I couldn't travel in the caves. With no other option, I ran to the water.

I didn't stop running until I was lifting off the ground.

Chapter 6

Wings ripped from my back and beat behind me as they carried me into the sky. My wings were heavy and tripled my arm's length on each side. They were made of the purest white feathers. Flying came naturally to me now that my form had presented itself to me. I felt like I could fly forever. But what was my form? My body was the same but I had massive white wings. I didn't know of any shifted form like that. Regardless, I was happy to shift and into a creature that could fly at that. I was finally free.

But where would I go? Considering the last two days of my life, where was I safe? I felt like a fugitive on the run trying to escape justice. I needed to see my best friend, Jude. She was born non-magic, in the middle caste, but had studied until she reunited with her power which had been dormant upon her birth. She was the smartest, most hard-working person I knew.

Jude was the firstborn of four. We grew up living within walking distance of each other but she went away to further her education at the Academy of Athena, a school for students who wanted to reignite the magic that lay dormant in their veins or study for a career. Naturally, Jude was doing both.

Jude had always been an exceptional student, working hard to make up for her lack of magic. And she had. She had willed magic into her veins like I had never seen before. We continued to write letters while she was away and she returned home each weekend, using her magic. Her magic and intelligence would come in handy right now, I thought to myself, as I flew through the sky.

I didn't know where I was going or what I would do when I got there. Surely I would still be hunted and I didn't want to put my father in danger. I needed to tell him what was going on though. I lived in the northern tip of the continent, beyond the Mountains of Boreas, so I would just fly north until I saw the mountains near my home, I guessed.

I was happy to be able to take a magical form enabled with flight, but was also slightly sad that I wouldn't be able to swim to the depths of the ocean. I had dreams as a child of being a mermaid, even though I knew that would be rare considering I was born in the Kingdom of Aether. Usually, citizen's shifted into forms that encompassed the elemental affinity of the Kingdom they were born into, but there were exceptions.

I had never flown before, and I should still be relishing in the freedom it gave me. But, after only flying for a short time, I was exhausted. My wings felt as though they were pulling me down towards the water. I had flown over the water, but along the sandy shores of the beach to keep track of where I was. It would have been a lot shorter for me to have flown over the water of the bay, but now I was thankful I hadn't. As the fatigue became overwhelming, I glided down to the sandy shore to take a break. I wasn't quite sure how to land, I felt like I was still gliding pretty fast. I put my feet down, attempting to hit the ground at a run, but tripped over a rock and tumbled.

I violently somersaulted until I came to a skid on the rocky, sandy surface of the beach. I landed on my side and glanced down at my cut-up, sandy body. My pants were torn and numerous cuts were bleeding. As the saltwater ebbed and flowed up the beach in small waves, the water reached me where I was laying in the sand. The saltwater should have burned my exposed flesh but instead, wherever it touched, my cuts disappeared. The water of the ocean was healing me.

That was odd because I hadn't taken the form of a creature of the water. I had wings so the water shouldn't call to me. I also wasn't a citizen of the Kingdom of Pontus. I looked down, frowning, watching the water healing my cuts and washing comfort over me. I was so thankful though.

Off in the distance, I could hear something approaching. I strained my ears until I heard the wheels of the carriage caravan that I had been a part of not too long ago. They were traveling through the woods on the side of the beach. I was exposed and I could only guess that they had seen me plummet out of the sky.

I heard the horses neigh and their hooves started hitting the ground harder. I scrambled but there was nowhere to hide, laying out in the open on the sand. I jumped to my feet, looking around for ideas.

Chapter 7

I wouldn't consider myself to be an excellent swimmer. If I swam out into the water, just in an attempt to escape, would they follow? I really didn't have any other options. I scrambled down the sand towards the water. I realized my wings were gone now that I was upright again.

My feet hit the wet sand as the water ebbed in and out. I continued running, picking my feet up to step over the water with each step in an attempt to go faster. It splashed as I ran, getting deeper. Soon the water was deep enough to cover my knees and then my hips. It swooshed as I cut through it. The water was creating a drag which was slowing me down. Once the water was crawling up my midsection, I dove into it. I began swimming away from the shore, throwing one hand in front of the other.

I heard shouts from the sandy beach and looked over my shoulder to see Declan standing there, demanding my return. Next to him, Jake stood smirking. He had his hands in his pockets. He looked calm and unbothered.

Jake had dark black hair that was shorn up the sides and longer on the top. He had sharp angles and his features looked dominating. Standing next to Declan, he looked like he could easily overpower him. He had such a confidence to him. He turned to Declan and frowned slightly as Declan screamed with rage beside him.

Declan approached the water and I cursed myself. He was a fucking siren. What the fuck was I thinking? I should've tried to fly again to escape. As I continued to paddle out into the water, I kept looking over my shoulder. Declan seemed to be unable to enter the water. He should've easily caught up to me by now but it seemed like he was forbidden.

A choppy wave broke in my face and I sank under the surface, gasping. Miraculously, it felt the same below the water as it had above. I was able to breathe easily. I kept swimming but in the direction that followed the curve of the beach. My feet felt bound together so I looked down quickly. There, I found my legs had been transformed into a beautiful green and purple fin from my waist down. I was shifted into a mermaid and all the dreams I had when I was a little girl were coming true. Except for the part where a psychopath was on the beach chasing me.

This didn't make sense though. I had never heard of anyone taking two shifted forms before. I looked down again to make sure I wasn't hallucinating. Maybe I was actually drowning and these were my last thoughts before I entered the afterlife. A few more moments passed and my beautiful fin was still there. I gave it a flick and it propelled me through the water with ease.

I didn't want to get out in the open water and not be able to find my way back. I just wanted to be home. I wanted to be with Jude. And I wanted things to make sense again. I had lived a simple life and I had been fine with it. I didn't understand any of this. I hadn't even begun to process how bad Declan's setup had stung. For now, I would just stay in shallow water and follow the shoreline north.

Suddenly, the sea got rough and I was swaying from side to side. I sunk to the bottom in an attempt to hide. A voice began to speak to me as if someone was right next to me. "Evelyn, you cannot run from me. I will never stop hunting you," Declan's voice boomed through the sea. I looked around but he was nowhere to be found.

I realized I had stopped swaying after his words found me

and the water slowly calmed. I had to get some space between Declan and me. His threat made goosebumps raise up and down my arms, even underwater. I decided to slowly move up to the surface and, as I inched closer and closer, I became more afraid of what I would find.

I broke the surface and looked around. My wet hair stuck to my face and I reached up and pushed it out of my eyes. I flicked my fin and paddled my arms to tread water as I searched the beach for them. Declan and Jake were no longer standing there so I had to assume they re-boarded the invisible caravan. They were probably planning to follow along the shore to wait for me to surface. Now that I knew Declan's intentions, I would have to make sure to always be looking over my shoulder.

I trod water for several moments with just my eyes above the surface. Fatigue was taking over me again so I decided to return to the shore to rest. I began swimming to the shore when something snagged my fin. I was pulled under the surface. I panicked and bubbles escaped my mouth. I took another breath and looked down.

A sea serpent's tail was wrapped around the narrow part of my fin tightly and its open mouth was moving toward me. The serpent's mouth was full of sharp teeth and its body was covered in green, hard scales. It had two sharp horns pointing backward on its head. Its eyes were white and empty.

I held out an outstretched hand on instinct and, begging the gods to save me, fire blasted from my hand hitting the sea serpent in the face. It shrieked and released me, taking off in the opposite direction. How the fuck did I do that? There was no time to sit here and think so I continued swimming toward shore and attempted to calm my pulse.

I noticed movement off in the distance. Curiosity took over and I swam towards it. I flipped my fin up and down and it propelled me quickly. As I got closer, the shape became clearer. A beautiful mermaid was ahead of me. She had long purple hair and a bright green fin. Her skin was pale and she was nude from the waist up. She was still in the water as if knowingly waiting for me.

"Legatum?" she asked.

"No, Evie," I corrected. "I'm trying to get back to the Kingdom of Aether, can you tell me the best way?" I asked. My voice sounded clear as if not surrounded by water. I expected communicating underwater to be different.

"You are being hunted?" she asked.

"I am," I replied, slowly. "How do you know that?" I asked.

"Legatum, you must master your gifts. You are the Lost Child and many will come for you. You must make ready," she added. "You need to visit the Oracle".

"Uh, ok," I said, not knowing what the hell she was talking about. "Where should I go from here?" I asked.

"Return to the shore and create a shelter to rest. You are very tired. Tomorrow you will travel North West to your home. You can shift into a form with wings and fly," she replied.

"And how is it I can take the form of a mermaid and of a flying beast?" I asked.

"Because you are a Legatum," she said, as if it was obvious. "You are not asking the right questions. I cannot give you the answers unless you ask the questions first," she added.

"Ok, well," I started. I had no idea what the hell was going on. "I'm not really sure what questions I need to ask," I finally said.

"When you know the questions, return to the Lagoon of Mermaids. Your answers will be there awaiting you. We will help you, Legatum," she finished and turned away. She darted off into the depths of the ocean.

Uh, ok. I would have to work that situation out later. Right now I was floating underwater, in the shifted form of a mermaid that had just been attacked by a sea serpent when I met another mermaid who would answer all my questions if I had any. Unfortunately, I couldn't think right now because I was being chased by a Duke of a Kingdom that was trying to give me to another Kingdom. Things were not going well. She told me to travel North West but I needed to travel North East to return to Aether, so maybe she didn't actually have all the answers.

I looked around to find the shore by the slope of the sea floor. I started to flip my tail to travel to more shallow water. Once it was shallow enough to walk, I willed myself back into Fae form, knowing that I could walk up to the shore now.

Soon I was able to touch the floor of the ocean with my feet. I made contact with the soft sand and used it to push off and propel myself forward. It became more and more shallow until I was walking with most of my body above the water, my wet clothes hanging off me. They were wet even though I had felt completely dry under the water. I was soon walking on the wet sandy beach with no direction. I collapsed for a moment to catch my breath and try to understand what had just happened. I was panting and a smile broke out on my face. Soon a laugh escaped me. I had just escaped death and I was thankful to the gods that I was still alive.

Remembering Declan's words, "I will never stop hunting you," I stood, panting and contemplating my next move. I wasn't sure where I was headed but I knew who I didn't want to run into along the way.

Message received Declan, you fucking piece of shit.

Chapter 8

I walked up the beach until the terrain below me changed. I kept walking, dripping water, my clothes hanging heavily off my body. I was sandy, sticky, and wet. I didn't even know the best route to get back to the Kingdom of Aether. I didn't know if I should move inland or follow the beach. I headed into the woods, for coverage, but stayed close enough to see water out in the distance. The woods got thicker and thicker as I continued to walk.

It was getting late and I needed to rest. What a day it had been. I had no money on a good day and now I was being hunted. I thought I was being transported to safety but today took an odd turn. Instead, I had been banished to the Caves of Echidna, crash-landed mid-flight, and been attacked by a sea serpent. At least there had been a lovely chat with a mermaid that made no sense. I hadn't really gotten to explore my power yet but it was there, thankfully, pulsing through my veins.

A breeze swirled around me. "Evelyn, do not wander the woods alone at night," the wind seemed to whisper in my ear. What the hell was that? It was clearly a male's voice and I spun around to see if anyone was near. My eyes darted around at the bushes and even up into the trees. No one was there and I was completely alone.

Maybe I could will something into place just for the night. If I had earth magic, I could make a cave similar to the one I watched Declan make the previous night. I held up my hands, going over what I had watched him do to create the cave. I squeezed my eyes closed, hoping to be able to create some kind of dwelling for the night, it didn't even need to be a cave just some place to shelter me.

After a few moments, with my eyes still squeezed tight, I peeked out. Nothing had formed in front of me. A noise in the distance startled me and I jumped. I looked in the direction of the noise and saw smoke billowing. I decided to run in the direction of the smoke thinking that there might be someone that would help me. The further I got from the water, the thicker the vegetation was.

I was running through vines and bushes. I had small cuts on my arms and even had tears in my clothing. I was stepping over branches and logs, trying to stay upright and leaves were crunching under my boots. The air was starting to cool and I was still damp but the chill helped to cool my body from the physical exertion.

After a while of running, it looked as though I was in a dense forest. It became harder to run so I slowed to a walk. While on uneven terrain, I was having to work harder to step over rocks, vines, and bushes. There were large trees every six to eight steps that I was wandering through.

I could hear all kinds of animals. I could hear crickets chirping and birds cawing. I could hear an owl cooing off in the distance. I could also hear growls and jowls snapping. I glanced over my shoulder continuously to see if anybody or anything was following me.

I slowed my steps, trying to travel quietly as I approached the dwelling that began to appear in a clearing of trees. Leaves were shuffling under my damp boots and, every so often, a limb snapped and made me jump. I came to the edge of the clearing. I could see a house off to what I assumed was the west side of the clearing, judging by the now setting sun. It was a large house with smoke rising out from the chimney.

Off a ways from the house, on the side of the hill, was a barn. The barn appeared to be tall enough to have a loft, which would make the perfect resting place for a fugitive such as me. I considered just approaching the house and asking for help. I didn't know who I was running from or what story to tell these people. I didn't even know who lived here. Mortals may turn me away for being Fae since there was tension from previous generations mistreating the mortals. If they were Fae, I could explain my story. But it sounded pretty mad and I wasn't really sure I understood it myself. I definitely would not invite a hysterical Fae that appeared out of nowhere into my home. I sighed and decided to stay with the original plan.

I followed the edge of the clearing, glancing in the direction of the house often, to avoid being seen. I also wanted to make sure no one was sneaking up on me. Once I reached the barn I would have to run, exposed for a short distance, to get to the entrance. I got close enough to risk the run out in the open and slowed to a stop.

I took one last look around to make sure that no one had wandered outside. Once I felt that there was no one around, I took off for the barn as quickly as my feet would carry me. I reached the door and yanked the handle hoping it would open. The door flung open, more easily than I had expected, and banged against the barn. I cursed quietly and lunged into the barn pulling the door closed behind me. I found a crack in the wood paneling of the door and peeked out to see if anyone was coming out to check the noise. After several long moments had passed, I relaxed and turned to try and find a ladder into the loft of the barn.

When I turned, I saw several stalls lining one side of the barn. The main part of the room housed several pieces of farm equipment. I could see tack gear hanging on the wall. I was familiar because of the time I spent working for the veterinarian. At the end of the stalls, I saw the ladder so I headed towards the far end of the room in its direction. It was getting dark outside now, so I was running my hand along with the stalls as I passed.

A horse's head popped up and it neighed and huffed, making me jump. The stalls had half doors and the horses all approached the hallway as if I was bringing them food. There were six large, beautiful horses poking their heads out over the stalls. They were snorting and stomping their feet. As I passed each one I gently ran my hand down its nose, studying their faces.

The first horse I passed was gentle and all white. I kept walking after stopping to pet the white horse for a few moments. I approached the next horse which was brown and calm as well. As I continued to walk, it nudged my shoulder as I passed. The third looked me in the eyes, begging me to stay with it. It was jet black and looked like the most spirited of the bunch. The horse pushed me with her nose then circled around her stall returning to me again. I smiled and kept walking. The fourth horse was brown with a white blaze. I rubbed its nose a few times and kept walking. The fifth was brown and white and stomped its front leg as I passed, jerking its head up and down. I didn't pet it many times because it seemed irritated. The last horse was brown and smaller than the rest. I guessed it to be a foal, less than one year of age. When it saw that I didn't have any food it turned and headed for the back of its stall and laid back down in the hay.

I had been assisting in the care of animals for the last four years. Working with animals came naturally to me. Had I had money, I could've joined Jude at the Academy of Athena and pursued a career in that myself. I hated school, but a job where I could work with animals was one thing I would endure it for. That and to spend more time with Jude. The only reason I worked was to have enough money to pay for our home in case my father was imprisoned or unable to work. The necessities, I had to nab from the local market. I had always been glad to have found the opportunity to work at a job that I enjoyed.

It wasn't common for a maiden to work, but more Fae than I had hoped knew of my father's habits and correctly assumed our situation. The veterinarian approached me one day and offered the job. She needed assistance around her farm and with the animals she was caring for since her husband had died. As I thought of my experiences working with the animals on her farm, a thought entered my mind. I could use one of these horses to get back to my town after I rested.

There were hooks with blankets hanging just by the stairs. Perfect. I grabbed a blanket and, even though it was covered in horsehair, I carried it with me. It was thick and heavy so I hoped it would combat the cold night.

To the right was a ladder that led up to the loft in the barn. I threw the blanket over my shoulder and put both hands on the ladder. I began climbing the ladder, my muscles aching from the day's events. When I reached the top, I stepped out onto a thin wooden board that acted as the floor of the loft. I undressed and hung my clothes to dry on nails that were sticking out of the wooden wall of the barn. I hoped that my clothing would be dry by the time I was ready to travel again. My stomach groaned and I realized that I hadn't eaten all day. That was a problem I would solve when I awoke again. I was so exhausted that I had barely been able to climb the stairs. I would just sit for a short while and rest my eyes. I grabbed the blanket and threw it over me.

Suddenly a rooster crowed loudly. I jolted awake, opening my eyes and realizing it was light outside again. I jumped to my feet as comprehension flooded my mind. For a fleeting moment, I had forgotten that I had been beaten, kidnapped, left at a cave prison, and threatened by a male I had made love to all in the last four days. I had slept like I had no cares in the world.

Thinking about Declan enraged me. Now that I knew he was a siren, everything made sense. I couldn't figure out if I had actually spent time with him in the weeks leading up to my capture or if he had placed false memories in my mind. Either way, everything that occurred when he was around was fake. When he neared me, I became overpowered with lust. That was just the power of his form and it wasn't actually how I had felt. I should've trusted my instincts when I thought of the feelings I felt in the memories.

In the memories he gave me, I was happy to be financially taken care of. Which was odd because I had never cared about money or the fact that I lacked it. I had always made do and I was fine with that. I didn't need some Prince Charming to come and rescue me. In the memories, I had felt relieved to not have to steal from the market. False again. As bad as it was, I enjoyed swiping items from the market in the same way I enjoyed chasing animals through the woods. I loved the thrill. Which reminded me of the false feelings he pushed into my mind when we fucked. He made me feel happy to satisfy him, seeking no satisfaction myself. That definitely wasn't me. I also wasn't a 'lay down and take it' type. I am combative even in the bedroom. I also seemed to bite my tongue around him. I had never bitten my tongue in my life and had been told, on more than one occasion, that I was a difficult female. The next time I saw that fucking asshole I was going to beat the shit out of him for it. I would need to learn to harness my elements by then.

I slid the blanket off my naked body, feeling the cold air all over my skin. As I stood to grab my clothes off of the nails, the barn door banged open. There was a board blocking me from view as if I was in a small, wooden cell with only three walls. I quietly slid my thin, dry sweater over my head and pushed my hands into the sleeves. I stepped quietly into my pants and pulled them up. I stuffed my foot into my boot, finding that it was still damp inside. I put the other boot on and tiptoed to the edge of the board blocking my view. I slowly peered around the board.

An older male had the all-black horse out of its stall, saddled, and ready to ride. He stood at her side, tightening the strap that was holding her saddle on. He cursed under his breath and said, "Hold on Lenore, I forgot the seeds up at the main house," and he turned and walked out of the barn.

If I wasn't fated to steal this horse, then I didn't know what fate was. It was like the gods gifted it to me. I ran down the stairs, missing a step and falling the last little ways. I landed on my ass but jumped up and ran to Lenore. I shoved one foot into the stirrup and, with a hop, threw my leg over her, landing in the saddle. I gave her a little kick and led her to the small, Fae-sized side doorway. I ducked but the door frame still scraped along my back. It caught the material of my sweater ripping it a little.

As we exited the barn, I heard the door at the main house squeak on its hinges. I kicked Lenore as hard as I could and darted towards the woods. I never turned back to see if the old male saw us leave or not.

We entered the trees and I dodged branches while trying to keep her at a quick pace. I looked around for a trail. There must be one because this male was obviously due to ride her. With no such luck, the ground started sloping downward slightly and I flung forward. Lenore flipped her head back to try to keep us from flipping over head first. She hopped with her back legs and stomped lightly to right us. I was sliding out of the saddle and let myself fall to the ground.

I walked around to her face. I didn't want to scare her and I wanted her to be obedient so I ran my hand down her face. "Sorry, Lenore. I'm Evie. Thank you for your help today," I said to her. She was all I had now and a frown pulled at my face. I kissed her lightly and then remembered I needed to get off this male's property before he came out looking for us. I looked around while I walked back to her side. I stepped back into the stirrup and hopped back up into the saddle. I saw a clearer area off ahead and I led her towards it. Once we got to the clearing, I saw several sandy paths heading in different directions.

I headed north, using the memory of where the sun set the night before. I sped up and ran Lenore like the wind for as long as I could. After a while, rain clouds rolled in and the rain began to fall. Perfect, I thought, and rolled my eyes. I had just dried out from yesterday. We kept charging forward though. Rain pelted me in the face and stung my eyes. Lenore didn't slow. It was like she enjoyed the run through the rain.

Finally, after we had run for what seemed like days, she slowed. The rain had stopped but we had trudged on. It was time to reward Lenore for her hard work. I looked around, seeing a stream up ahead.

We had traveled a good distance and I no longer feared that Lenore's owner would find us. I just needed to watch out for other threats now.

I kicked my leg over the saddle and slid down to the ground. I took Lenore by the reins and led her to a small creek. She bent down and drank and drank. I patted her back and rubbed her neck. While she was drinking, I leaned down and cupped my hands to drink myself. I realized how thirsty I was and quickly drank six handfuls before I could slow down.

I looked around to see if there were any edible plants and lucked up when I found a berry bush. I grabbed several and threw them in my mouth before grabbing another handful for Lenore. She ate them greedily too and I realized that Lenore and I were going to get along just fine. I smiled, running my hands down her neck. She was a kindred spirit. She turned her head and started plucking berries off of the bush herself.

After a few moments of rest, and a deep exhale, I grabbed Lenore's reins and led her back to a clearer path. I walked alongside her for several moments. My arm was under her neck and I ran my hand down her soft fur. I turned to look at her and her gentle eyes flicked to me. I smiled at her and was so thankful for her company. A tear slid down my cheek and she turned her head and nudged me on the shoulder. It was almost as if she was comforting me. I stopped and faced her. She turned her neck to me and I hugged her. She tucked her neck over my shoulder and huffed snot all over me. I laughed and ran my hand down both sides of her neck. I stepped back and walked back to her side.

I stepped into the stirrup and, with a hop, slung my leg back over the saddle. I urged her forward but less aggressively than before. She took off at a run like she just enjoyed running. I laughed and let her run for a long time. Eventually, she tired and slowed to a trot. As she slowly trotted along the path, we approached a clearing.

Off in the distance, I could see the foot of a mountain, a mountain I recognized. My mouth dropped open. I guess Lenore had traveled much faster at a run than the caravan had at its slow, walking pace.

We were back in the Kingdom of Aether at the base of the Mountains of Boreas, God of the North Wind. My home.

Chapter 9

Father and I resided just on the other side of the third mountain from the coast in a long stretch of mountains. I had read in a book that there was a winding path that led from our village out past this mountain for travelers that were heading to the Kingdom of Pontus.

As we got closer, I could make out the clear, well-traveled path and guided Lenore to it. I hoped that we could complete our journey before sunset. We sauntered down the path and I started feeling like I was being watched. I looked around cautiously but saw no one. Since my status had changed from a free woman to a hunted fugitive, I had to keep checking over my shoulder.

A breeze swirled around me, and like a whisper in my ear, a soft voice said, "Do not return to the prison." I snapped my head around, pulling Lenore's reins and we spun in a circle. There was no one around, especially not anyone who could've whispered to me.

I had to go to the prison. I had to see my father. I still was unsure of what I would say to him because I didn't want him to get upset while being imprisoned. There was nothing he could do anyway but worry. I just needed to see a familiar face and figure out where to go from here. I didn't suppose I should return to my town.

Lenore continued to trot as we wound around the second mountain. I heard a rustling over to one side. I snapped my head in the direction as I heard a roar. Lenore took off, and I turned to look over my shoulder. A small brown cat-like animal was tearing after us. I had nothing to fight the animal with. I cursed myself for not finding some type of weapon before leaving Lenore's barn. Fuck. I tightened my legs around Lenore as I moved up and down in the saddle. I was trying hard not to fall off, and silently panicked, I threw my hand behind me. Fire shot out of my hand again, and the beast yelped. It jumped over the fire, slowing just a bit, and was back at it. I tried again, begging the gods to spare my life. I had been stupid to think I could travel all this way without needing any type of protection. I reshot fire, but the beast expected it and dodged the stream of fire.

Then the beast leapt into the air and made contact with Lenore's hind leg. The horse stumbled and fell to the ground and I went down with her. In a panic, I begged for a weapon and a knife appeared in my hand. My jaw dropped, and I looked up to find the beast's jaws locked on Lenore's leg. I threw the knife, like a dart, at the beast's face. It landed in its eye, killing it instantly. I sat there on the ground, panting heavily. Lenore had a nasty gash on her leg.

I looked down at my sweater. The back half was shredded anyways. I ripped off the loose fabric and it tore the bottom half of the sweater off. It wasn't enough so I found a tear in one of the sleeves and ripped the sleeve off. I moved to rip the other sleeve off too to create makeshift ties. I was left with barely enough fabric to cover my breasts.

I held the fabric on her leg and used the sleeves to tie it tightly like I had seen the veterinarian do. I jumped up and walked around to her face. I bent down and comforted her. "I'm so sorry, Lenore," I said, laying on her neck. She huffed and started pushing herself up. My eyebrows raised as she slowly stood. She took a couple of practice steps and then stomped her back foot. I walked to her face and ran my hands down it again. I looked into her gentle eyes and smiled warmly. She nudged me in the chest, encouraging me to get back on. I laughed and jumped back into the saddle.

We trotted on and, finally, started to bend around the third mountain. Off in the distance, I saw vast plumes of smoke. I strained my vision to make out what was on fire. Now that I was a Fae with activated powers, my vision was sharper than it had been. I gasped as I realized what was now burnt to the ground. My entire village of Ventus was gone, replaced with smoke and ash.

I was frozen with fear, shock, and sadness. I halted Lenore while a tear ran down my cheek. Who had fucking done this? Could it have been Declan? Had he known I would return here? Of course I would return here, where else would I have gone? I tried to piece together my thoughts. How had he made it here so quickly? I hoped my father was still in prison. Our village was so small that they housed the criminals in a town nearby. I tried to recall whether Declan knew where my father was imprisoned or not. I couldn't remember if we had spoken about it.

I thought of Jude and her family and tears started to spill from my eyes. What day was it? Had she returned home or would she still be safe at school? Then I thought of her three younger siblings and her parents and more tears came as I choked out a sob.

I thought of my friends and Fae I knew. I frequented the same places often and, even though I tried to avoid others, had a few Fae that I regularly engaged in conversation with.

I also thought of the male, Luke, whom I had been casually seeing but was not in a relationship with. However, my heart ached at the possibility of his passing. He was my age and we had gone to school together our whole lives. He was the first person I slept with and, even though it wasn't great, we had continued to meet up regularly. He wasn't the best but we got along and it was something to do. Plus, he was one of my good friends. Tears were spilling down my cheeks now. Lenore trotted on.

A shiver ran down my spine, and a nagging feeling that I was being watched came over me again. I needed to leave this place. I needed to find somewhere safe to stay the night. It wasn't safe for me to be out here alone in the dark. I started racking my brain for ideas. The next town wasn't much further, I would head there and try to find somewhere to hide out for the night.

I kicked Lenore's sides to see if she could run. She didn't hesitate and she sped off. We headed to the town of Aer, to the prison where my father was being kept.

Chapter 10

I approached the prison, sooner than expected. My head was still swimming with thoughts and I had run out of tears. I solidified the questions I would ask my father and decided to keep what I could to myself. This was certainly a conversation I never expected to have with him. My tears had dried on the side of my face as I had continued to cry long into the ride. I reached up and wiped my face. I needed to appear as normal as possible.

I was close enough to the building now to swing my leg over Lenore and slide to the ground. I led her to the side of the building and tied her off. I ran my hand down her face several times then headed toward the prison. I walked up to the door, pausing as I reached for the handle, remembering that I was barely dressed. I looked around, having no other options. I took a deep breath and released it slowly before yanking the door open.

I walked into the prison and was met by a familiar face. I had been here before, more times than I could count, to visit my father. The male stood and recognized me. His gaze dropped to my exposed stomach and shot back up to my face. He didn't seem too disturbed. He was an older male, wearing glasses, and had been reading something on the desk in front of him. He offered me a half-smile as he stood. He grabbed a key and led the way to the cells in the back of the building. He started to usher me down the dark, dusty hallway like this was our typical routine. He didn't even need to ask who I was here to see.

The hallway was lit by candles that hung from the ceiling every few steps. Not many Fae were housed here. Most went off to the big prison, central to the kingdom, but this small jail housed the lesser criminals. My father was, usually, serving time for being a drunkard, which wasn't the absolute worst thing, I guessed.

We got to my father's cell, where he was laying down on his back on the floor snoring. "Father," I said, my voice breaking. He continued to snore so I repeated myself twice before he awoke slowly. He pushed himself into a sitting position on the dusty floor.

"Evie, hello darling," he said, excitedly. "And happy birthday!" he finished. "I'm going to change my ways upon my release, you'll see," he promised. I smiled tightly, as I did every time he made these promises. He looked down to what I was wearing but didn't seem bothered much by it either. "Oh! Have your powers revealed themselves to you?" he asked excitedly.

"A little. But that's not what I came by to discuss with you father," I let out a sigh as I sat down on the dusty floor outside of the cell bars. I pulled my knees up, crossing them in front of me as my father shifted to mimic me. He scooted himself so that we were almost sitting knee to knee, the bars separating us.

My father was a heavyset male with brown curly hair that hung to his chin and he had deep brown eyes. In contrast, I had straight brown hair and bright, turquoise eyes. He had a round nose and I had a thin nose. We actually couldn't look more opposite now that I thought about it.

"What is it, my sweet Evie?" he asked warmly. Father had many shortcomings but loving me was not one.

I didn't want to worry my father while he was stuck in here so I had to be careful about what I said. I couldn't tell him that I had been kidnapped because he would go mad with worry. I couldn't tell him about traveling back from the Caves of Echidna because that would raise even more questions. I decided to keep it as simple as possible, omitting most of the story.

I felt unease and nervousness wash over me like I needed to

leave this place. Worry pulled at my gut even though I wanted to sit here with my father all night. I needed to ask my questions quickly so I could find somewhere to stay the night.

"Do you know of anyone who would try to hurt me, Father?" I asked, trying to sound calm.

Father stiffened, "What's happened, Evie?" he demanded.

There was really no way around it. Father and I did not bullshit with each other. I would tell some truths but downplay them. Once father was released, I would fill him in on the whole story. He would understand why I withheld the truth from him and he would forgive me.

"Well, someone approached me in town and told me I was in trouble. Then a couple of days later, today, the town burned down," my voice got quieter with every word I spoke.

"WHAT?" father yelled. "I have to get out of here to help the survivors. Evie, you could've been killed! I am so glad you're ok," he said as he reached through the bars to cup my face. He had on a pair of magic binding gloves, preventing him from bending his fingers, which he seemed to have forgotten.

I leaned into his embrace, nonetheless. Anxiety was building and I knew I needed to go. I was running out of time. "Father, the Fae implied you were not, well, that you are not my biological father," I said casually, trying not to hurt him with my words.

Father's eyes grew large and he remained stock still for several moments. He broke my gaze and his eyes slowly drifted down while darting around the room. "Well, I am not sure how they could've known that. Evie, it was never something I meant to hide. Your mother brought you home one day and she died within a few years and we had never really discussed how to tell you and-" he began to ramble.

I cut him off, "Wait, so it's true? You're not my actual father?" I was horrified. I wanted him to be my father. I wanted all of this to be a misunderstanding. Even with all of his shortcomings, when we were together, we were happy. He was fun and fun-loving, which is what got him into trouble most of the time. When I got in trouble, he shrugged it off. He never came down hard on me, no matter what I had done. He was supportive and loving in his own way.

"Ok," he said, letting out a long breath, "Let me start from the beginning." I waited with my eyebrows raised. I tried to mask my shock knowing that this would change nothing between us. At least, I hoped it wouldn't.

He began again staring off into empty space like he was reminiscing of a better time, "Your mother and I tried for years to have a baby, you see. We really had given up all hope. She had gone to see her friend from school who lived near the Palace of the King and Queen. She was gone for a few days." He chuckled lightly then continued, "One day, she turned up holding a baby. I said, 'Jane, who's baby have you stolen now?' and laughed but she didn't return my lightheartedness. She just stood there, stock-still. I asked again, 'Jane? Who's baby do you have?' and she responded with one word, 'Ours.' I ushered her into our home and we sat down on the bed. She went into the full story of what had happened," he said, continuing.

"She told me that she had been down to the market with her friend. On the way home, she stopped by a stream to get a drink of water after collecting items all day. She bent down to take a drink and heard a baby crying. She crossed the stream and followed it, just a few steps, before she saw a baby in a basket. You had floated down a stream until it was no longer deep enough to carry the weight of a baby in a basket. She picked you up and looked around but no one was there. She knew it was a gift from the gods. The gods had given you to us. You were her most prized possession. When she got sick, she worried about you day and night. I can still hear her crying on my shoulder when she got sick, knowing she would surely pass and miss out on the life you still had to live." Tears were flowing down my father's cheeks. I reached a hand up to wipe my face, noticing that they were flowing down my cheeks too.

He finally met my gaze again, "But I have never, for one second, felt that you weren't my daughter, Evie. Not one second."

I nodded quickly, "Thank you, Father. For caring for me and loving me."

"I'm really going to do better this time, Evie, I promise. Losing your mother was the hardest thing," he choked on a sob.

"I know, Father. It's ok," I said, meaning it. "I don't have a lot of time before I need to go. I am going to travel to see Jude since we no longer have a home here. Is there anything else that you can tell me that may be helpful to me on my journey?" I asked.

"Oh yes, Evie. First, go into town and tell Lucas he needs to accompany you to the Academy of Athena," Father started. I recoiled visibly. I hadn't spent much time with Lucas in recent years. Lucas was just a tall, lanky boy I played with as a child who was annoying as hell. Our fathers were friends and had known each other since they were children. We had spent a good amount of time with Lucas' family until the last several years, when my father's drinking had really picked up.

"But, Father-" I interrupted.

He cut me off again, "I don't want to hear it, Evie. You're not traveling halfway across the continent alone." I sighed. I knew I had done just that to get here but I was going to leave that part out of this conversation.

"Go to Lucas, give him a chance. You aren't children anymore. Tell him I said you need assistance in my absence and that I will make this up to him. I will figure out a way to repay him. Then, you will need to go to the Oracle for your ring," he said bossily.

Oh right. I had been so distracted that I had forgotten that every Fae visited the Oracle upon their twenty-first birthday or shortly thereafter. I needed to get my custom-made power ring to replenish my power after using it. That would be critical.

I started to hear a lot of noise outside and I instinctively jumped to my feet. My father mimicked my movements, "Evie you should go. Get Lucas. I get out of here tomorrow and will return to our town to try and help where I can. Send word that you are ok along the way," he said, peering down the hall.

Puzzled, "What do you mean? How can I send word?" I asked.

"Speak your message onto a breeze, tell the wind to bring it to your Father. The wind will listen to you, Evie. You are a citizen of the Kingdom of Aether. The wind will be your strongest elemental affinity," Father said confidently as if he suddenly knew that to be true. How could he know that, I wondered?

I heard Lenore neigh loudly outside. My head darted in the direction of the noise then back to my father. I reached through the bars and then pulled him in for a hug. He pressed his face between two bars to plant a kiss on my cheek. I turned to face him and said, "I love you, Father. Please take care."

He nodded then replied, "I love you too Evie, my strong, beautiful girl." He reached up and lightly knocked my chin with the back of his gloved hand. I turned from him and started walking back the way I came, to the prison door. I looked down at the thin fabric barely covering my busty frame. It was sliding up and I pulled it down, still revealing my entire stomach. I just needed to get to Lucas' home and then I could borrow a shirt from his sister.

Through a small window, I caught a glimpse of Declan and his armored guards holding Lenore's reins and looking her over. One pointed at her leg, wrapped in the sweater I had been wearing. I cursed under my breath. I could slip out the door and around the back of the building but now, I would lose Lenore. Luckily, Lucas' house was within walking, well running, distance from here.

I waited until their backs were turned to me and asked the prison worker to forget I had been here. He gave me a confused look then looked out the window to see all the males there. He looked back at me and nodded. "Be careful," he whispered. I nodded, then slipped out the door.

I slowly crept around to the side of the building and then turned to run to the back. The cold air had covered me in goosebumps. As I hit the corner of the building, someone grabbed my wrist, and I crashed into a hard body.

I looked up into my assailant's face, recognizing Jake, and felt lightning crash through me. My wrist sparked and crackled where he touched me. I gasped. We were sharing breaths and I was panting. We stayed that way for a few moments. I wasn't sure what to do. I couldn't yell for help. I couldn't run because of his tight grip.

He was so tall pressed this close to me, and his black hair flipped over a cowlick to one side. My eyes ran over his face. His eyes were bright green, and his cheekbones were high and sharp. He had a thin pointed nose and a strong chin. His face was... perfect? He looked from my eyes down to my lips as I spoke.

My brows pinched. "Please," I whispered. I continued to beg, "Please, let me go." I was close enough to kiss him now. I was panicking, searching his face for a hint of sympathy. If he returned me to Declan, I was afraid of what would happen to me. Declan would be furious and most likely take it out on me up until the point where he threw me in the Caves of Echidna. I wasn't sure I would be able to escape the caves again. Jake was looking into my eyes, and his gaze dropped to my body and returned to my face.

"He's not the true Duke," he whispered. He let go of my wrist slowly and stepped back. He pulled his shirt off over his head by the neck, revealing his impressively muscular body. He had layers and layers of rippling muscle. He was covered in tattoos from his neckline to the waist of his pants and down his arms to his wrists. My gaze raked over his body. He grabbed my wrist, pulling me from the trance, and shoved his shirt into my hand. Then he walked past me as if he hadn't seen me. I rubbed where his tight grip had been. It felt tingly and warm even though he had had a tight hold of me.

I stood, frozen. I slowly turned around at the waist, not moving my feet. As he approached the front of the building, he yelled to the others, "Nothing back here." My mouth dropped open. Why did he do that for me? I threw his shirt over my head, my mouth open in shock. I was sure that his capture meant doom for me, but instead, he had spared me.

"I got blood on it while I was hunting," I heard him say. I guessed someone asked him where his shirt was. I couldn't get the image of his body out of my mind. Holy gods.

I swiveled back, facing the direction I was going, and ran for the tree line. I just needed to get under the cover of the thick forest, and then I could follow the tree line to Lucas' house.

Chapter 11

I crept along in a somewhat crouched position, trying not to cause a raucous. It was dark now and the noises coming from the forest set me on edge. I had been told growing up that there were animals that kept to the woods and hunted Fae. It was hard to tell what stories were old wives' tales told to keep children out of the forest or if there was truth to them. I didn't want to find out. I crept along as close to the edge of the woods as possible. I was nervously checking over my shoulder for animals, looking for Declan, and trying to run as quietly as I could.

Lucas' small home came into view, and I began to feel relieved. There was a fire inside the harth that I could see flickering through an open window. I was so close now; if I could just make it a little farther and get into Lucas' house.

As I took my next step, I was snatched backward and thrown to the forest floor. Leaves crashed and slid around me. I felt hands pinning me down by my shoulders, and claws dug into the shirt Jake had given me, piercing my skin.

I must've closed my eyes on impact, but I saw nothing but teeth as they flung open. The monster that pinned me down was on all fours over me. Its fur was gray, and it had a long, pointed snout lined with sharp pointy teeth. It had bright yellow eyes with large black pupils. It was salivating and panting, with thick drool dripping on my body from its jowls. It growled in my face with its sharp teeth clenched. It's breath fucking reeked, making me naseous.

I tried to push the animal off me, but it had me pinned to

the forest floor by my shoulders, not allowing a full range of movement. It snapped its jowls in my face as I used all of my strength to hold it back. I gave the gods a silent plea for help as I feared for my life. The large rat-like animal flew off of me and was thrown into a tree. It yelped as it hit the ground, looking back at me and shuffling to its feet. I watched as it ran off on all fours.

I lay panting. Had I just used the air with such force to knock a beast off of me and into a tree? This use of the elements was new to me but it seemed as though when I really wanted something, the gods listened to my inner thoughts. They responded to me in my desperation.

Scared to lay in the woods another moment, I pushed myself up into a sitting position and jumped to my feet. I broke the clearing and ran for Lucas' house, stumbling a little, tripped up by my own speed. As a Fae, I would have increased abilities now. I guess my speed was now heightened, and I would have to learn how to adjust to my new gifts.

The creature had torn my oversized shirt a little. I figured I looked nearly dead by now. My skin was exposed again and I was covered in scrapes from running through the woods the night before. I was covered in dirt and sweat. I had been on a long journey with no resources. But I was still moving forward and would continue.

I decided to run around to the front of the house and knock on the door, like a normal person, instead of appearing in the window like a frantic, wild female. I took a second to steady myself at the door and catch my breath before I knocked lightly, reeling in my fear. I started attempting to smooth down my long brown hair with my hands.

A few moments passed, and Lucas opened the door. He looked shocked. "Evie!" he exclaimed. "You're ok!" he said as if relieved.

How had he known about what had happened to me? Oh wait, he was referring to the fire in my town as if I had been there instead of kidnapped and fleeing for my life. Right, of course. He crushed me in a tight hug, glad I had survived. I hugged him back awkwardly. This was going to be quite the story to try to explain. Would he even believe me?

"Come in," Lucas said as he stepped aside and opened the door wide.

"Oh, thank you," I said, looking around for his parents. "Where are your parents?" I asked, surprised not to see them in the small space.

Lucas' home was much like mine and my Father's. There was one additional room, but they were still spread thin, having six children. Lucas was the oldest, so he and his closest sibling in age slept in the main room by the fire. The newest child slept in the room with Lucas' parents. The three school-aged children shared the other bedroom, barely large enough for the bed.

Lucas was three years older than me, and I hadn't seen him in a long time. Sometimes we ran into each other at the market, but it was nothing of a visit. We usually just waved, as we were both busy and didn't have much in common anymore. Now that we were up close, I could see that he had really grown and was well built. His body looked sturdy and strong and was lined with muscles. Everything else about him remained the same.

Lucas led me over to sit on a couch by the fire. His closest sibling, Claudia, was in the kitchen cleaning up after dinner. The youngest four must've already headed off to bed.

"Lucas," I exclaimed, unsure of where to start. "I have a lot going on right now, and I need your help." I got out.

"I know, I am so sorry about the fire. We can go tomorrow to see if there were any survivors or if we can salvage anything from your home," he said

I let out a long, slow breath. I was just going to say it. "Lucas, I was kidnapped four days ago by the Duke of Pontus, well maybe he's not the Duke according to his vampire guard, but now he's hunting me because he says I'm the Duchess of the Lost Realm. But I escaped at the Caves of Echidna, and I made it back here to confirm that Thomas isn't my actual father, but now I need to go to the Oracle," I barely stopped to take a breath.

Lucas' eyes were wide as he stared at me. A long, awkward silence passed, and he just stared at me, not even blinking.

"Please say something," I said lightly.

Lucas seemed to snap out of it. He shook his head lightly, and his eyebrows shot up. He exhaled slowly. "So, what's the plan then?" Lucas said, fully committed to this insanity. I was shocked. I had not been sure of his reaction during my entire journey here, and now, within moments, Lucas was fully committed and ready to leap off this cliff with me.

"Father said I needed to come and get you and then head to the Oracle to get my power ring," as I said it, I looked down to see his ring on the middle finger of his right hand. "I also want to go to the Academy to see Jude once I have my power ring," I continued. "I feel confident that Jude will know what to do," I said, trying to convince myself. I was nervously wringing my hands now.

Lucas and I sat angled in towards each other, with our knees touching. Lucas had been a longtime friend, so maybe my Father had a point in taking Lucas with me. He could at least offer me additional protection, I considered.

"Alright then," Lucas said without missing a beat. I couldn't believe that he was just going to drop everything and believe this crazy story I had just told him and go along for the ride. "My mother made supper before she left. Would you like a bite to eat before we travel?" he asked.

"Travel tonight?" I asked. He stood and offered his hand. I let him pull me up to stand at his side and I walked the few steps into the kitchen at his side.

Claudia offered me a small smile as she hung a rag on the side of the wash bin and walked out of the kitchen and into the bedroom where the youngest slept with their parents.

"Sure, if you are up for it. We can travel by Pegasus feather," he said. I hadn't thought about that. That would surely be easier than a trek across the continent.

A Pegasus feather carried the power of travel. When gifted to an individual by a Pegasus, the individual simply had to light the feather on fire, say where they wanted to go, and with a clap of magic, be transported to wherever they wished. Pegasuses weren't as common anymore so the feathers were hard to come by. As luck would have it, Lucas' mother was a Pegasus and gifted him with as many feathers as he liked. Lucas walked over to a cabinet, slid out a drawer, grabbed a bulging drawstring bag, and held it up with a smile. "Shall I take the whole bag?" he asked, grinning.

A smile lit my face and I replied, "Yes, please!" Ok, so father had a point about coming to get Lucas. Lucas was dedicated and resourceful.

Had Lucas been a Pegasus himself, the bag wouldn't be necessary but he had taken after his father. Lucas was of the Griffon form, which had perks of its own. He had speed, precision eyesight, and when shifted, large wings. Griffons benefited from having the head and wings of an eagle and the strong legs of a lion.

I grabbed a plate from the side of the wash bin, and loaded it with real food. I had been living off of berries and plants for days and I was salivating at the thought of putting something of substance in my mouth.

I sat down at the table and began to inhale the meal. Even when I had home-cooked food, it wasn't this good. One taste of the venison reminded me of what actual protein tasted like. I moaned as I closed my eyes, savoring every bite. After I finished the venison, I ate a huge helping of mashed potatoes and then green beans.

Lucas' family grew what they could but, due to the cold weather most of the year, they relied on the imports at the market. Luckily for them, both parents had sufficient jobs. His mother and father were both employed at the city center. It was a well sought after job. They lived modestly to ensure that their children had everything they needed. There was a tiny speck of envy in me but I was happy for them, nonetheless.

When I finished, I dropped my hands to my side and said, "Wow, Lucas. Your mother is an excellent cook." I was so full I was almost sick. I was also immediately tired. I just wanted to crawl up on their couch and go to sleep. But there was still a lot to do and I needed to get to Jude as soon as possible.

He smiled with a glimmer of pity in his eyes. He knew I had lost my mother and he knew that my father was a drunkard. Everyone knew. I'm sure he could tell that I didn't often eat food like this. I had a thin, toned body because I had to work for all the food I ate.

Lucas walked over to a small chest next to the couch he slept on. He opened it and took a few outfits out. He grabbed a drawstring bag and threw the clothes in, then slung the bag over his shoulder.

"I think I want to slightly change plans," I said, as I cocked a sly smile.

"I already predicted this and I'm not even a Sphinx," he replied, then laughed. I laughed too knowing that a Sphinx was able to read Faes' minds.

He pulled a feather out of the bag, slipping the bag into his pocket. He called out to his sister, telling her he was going on a journey with me to the Oracle of Isla. He grabbed my hand and led me to the fire in the fireplace. He looked at me and I nodded.

He leaned towards the fire, catching the Pegasus feather alight. He stood back up and said, "To the Academy of Athena." A loud clap snapped in my ears and his home flashed out of view.

Chapter 12

It was as if I had blinked, and suddenly we were standing in the lobby of the main building of the Academy of Athena. Pegasus' feathers were the fastest way to travel. Fae could be transported across the kingdom in the time it took to blink an eye.

I stood in awe. We were standing in a massive room with high ceilings. I had never been inside such an ornate structure. It was made of immaculate, smooth stone with white and gray swirls. The room was in the shape of a huge circle with five perfectly spaced hallways jutting off in different directions, opposite the main entrance. Overhead, it looked like there were illuminated icicles hanging from the ceiling but in one big clump.

"It's called a chandelier," Lucas leaned over and said quietly. I realized my mouth was gaping open and I slowly closed it and swallowed. The room was lit, but not with torches. It wasn't fire, it was an unchanging light. "They have electricity here," Lucas added. "It's fire magic that has been contained in a glass sphere. They have them all throughout this building and outside," Lucas said matter-of-factly.

I stood there speechless, taking it all in. I pointed at the walls, unable to form words. "It's called Marble," Lucas said, knowing my question. "The smartest, most gifted Fae have all passed through this school or have been drawn here for work. There are things here that can't be found anywhere else, except the Palace of the King and Queen of the royal Kingdom of Chaos. It is a place for advancements in many aspects of life," he said proudly.

"Holy shit," were the only words I could form and force from my mouth. Lucas laughed, sounding somewhat caught off guard.

"Come on, let's go find Jude," he grabbed my hand and started dragging me along. Thankfully, he guided me because I was still gawking at the structure we were in. The walls, the floors, and the high ceilings were all polished and gleaming.

A tall figure approached us, heels clicking on the elegant floor. She was tall and thin, and when I turned to her I had to throw a lot of concentration into not gawking. She was gorgeous. She had tan skin and her breasts were pushed up as though they would overflow out of her tight, strapless leather top. She had long blonde hair down to her waist. Her fingernails were long and painted bright red to match her lipstick. She had a short black leather skirt on and wore high black heels.

"Looking for someone?" she hissed, and I could almost hear her need for sex dripping off her tongue. She looked Lucas up and down like she wanted to devour him. Lucas was looking her up and down too, his gaze snagged on her breasts.

"Yes," I cleared my throat and flushed. "We are looking for Jude Rowan," although I started wondering if I could be best friends with this female instead.

"Second hallway, with the other wanna-be medical physicians. Last door on the right," she said enunciating every word. She looked at Lucas and smiled. He smiled back, doe-eyed. She took a few steps to close the distance between them. She placed her hands on Lucas' shoulders and he slid his hands onto her waist.

"Thanks," Lucas said, entranced. She leaned forward and pressed her red-painted lips onto Lucas' cheek. When she pulled back, he had a red kiss on his cheek. I stepped forward and grabbed his arm, pulling him away from her. He looked at me like he would die without this female.

"I'm in the third hall, last door on the right," she purred to Lucas. She sashayed away as I continued to drag Lucas in the opposite direction. As we got some distance between us, Lucas' face slowly returned to normal losing the entranced look he had had.

Lucas leaned in and whispered, "I'm a sucker for a succubus." Lucas chuckled while jabbing his elbow into my side. Even I shook my head trying to get out of the female's snare.

We walked down the wide hallway with an arched ceiling passing several windows. We got to the end of the hallway and stood before the door. We knocked lightly. I could hear two people giggling and shuffling around, knocking things over and giggling some more.

After a moment someone approached the door while shushing the other. Jude cracked the door just revealing the right half of her body. I could see she had on a knee-length, light pink robe. She obviously wasn't ready for visitors, because we had come over unannounced. I guess it was pretty late but she had been up because I had heard her from the hallway. Her long curly hair was frizzy and she looked disheveled. She was also out of breath. Realization flooded over me. Oh no.

Once she realized who stood in the hallway she pushed the door all the way open and yelled, "Evie!" As she ran forward and pulled me in for a tight embrace, I saw a male scrambling to pull on pants behind her, hopping on one foot while trying to shove another foot into the other leg hole. With Jude's back to her room, I was getting a show. She pulled back to look at me and saw my eyes snagged on the guy in the room. "Oh!" she exclaimed and blushed. She laughed lightly and turned, holding up her hands as if presenting this half-naked, actually mostly naked, male to us. "This is Beckett," she said as my eyebrows rose. I felt like I knew a lot about Beckett and his muscular body already. Beckett had finally gotten his second leg in and was pulling his pants up to his waist.

"Hi," Beckett said with a smolder, running his fingers through his ear-length blonde hair and pushing it to one side.

"Lucas?" Jude said, turning to Lucas. It had probably been even longer since Jude had seen Lucas because she was away most of the time.

"Hey Jude, it's been a long time," he said with a smile. Jude stepped past me and pulled Lucas into a hug. As she lifted her arms to wrap them around Lucas' neck, her nightgown rode up and caught half-naked, Beckett's, eye. Beckett cocked his head and smiled, realizing I was watching.

"Jude, I am so sorry to just show up like this but a lot has happened and I was wondering if we could talk," I asked looking from her to Beckett, raising my brows, to let her know I needed her alone. Beckett needed to go. I stood there in Jake's oversized shirt and Jude seemed to notice my disheveled appearance for the first time. She shrugged and turned towards Beckett.

Without a moment of hesitation, she walked over to Beckett, kissed him, looped her arm in his, and walked him to the door. "Bye babe," she said sweetly while Beckett, now in the hallway, searched for words. Jude turned from him and grabbed me by the elbow, holding her arm out for Lucas to grab the other. She threw Beckett a, "sorry" and led Lucas and me into her room. As she began to shut the door she saw Beckett's shirt on the floor. She walked over and picked it up, returning to the door. When she opened the door again, I heard Beckett say from the hallway, "Hey, what's going on-". Before he could finish Jude tossed him the shirt and shut the door, walking towards us smiling.

I laughed, then Lucas laughed, causing Jude to laugh. We all started laughing again and again at the awkwardness of the situation we had all just gotten ourselves into.

"Jude, it's so good to see you but I bring bad news," as I said the words, everyone's smile dropped. "Jude, I'm so sorry but Ventus burned down." It was hard to utter the words as if they sealed the fate of our little town. "Aer still stands," I added and Lucas slowly nodded his head knowing his town was safe. I continued, "I may be responsible."

Trying to take it all in Jude's eyes widened. After a few moments, Jude said with a shocked expression, "Oh my, what have you done now, Evie?" A tear rolled down Jude's cheek.

I walked over and sat on the little couch at the front of her room along the wall. "Let me start at the beginning, Jude," I said. Jude came and sat next to me. Lucas pulled up a chair. I began to run through the events. I gave a more detailed explanation than I had given Lucas initially. Lucas occasionally said, "Ah." like everything suddenly made sense now that I was filling in the gaps from the quick explanation I had given him back at his home in Aer.

Jude was seated next to me, our bodies angled towards one another, with our hands in our laps. Jude picked up my hand and squeezed it between her hands and I leaned toward her putting my head on her shoulder. "I don't know what to do Jude," I whispered. It was the first time I had really admitted to myself that I had no idea what the fuck I was doing or what I was going to do. I told her what Declan had said and all the details of how I got back to Ventus and then traveled to Aer to speak with my father. She seemed empathetic when she needed to be and was shocked during other parts of the story. After I finished the story, I took a long deep breath. I felt so much better just having my best friend here and her knowing everything I had been going through.

Lucas sat in a chair near a desk up against the opposing wall. The room was long and just wide enough to be able to access her bed from either side. Towards the front of her room was her, I assumed, school desk with a chair. The desk was neat and tidy with a stack of thick books shoved up against the wall. I looked down at the floor to see a stack of papers and writing supplies. I realized Jude and Beckett must've cleared the desk off while he was here, to fuck. Across from the desk, there was the worn brown couch three cushions wide, that we sat on. The room was small, but it worked. In the corner was a wardrobe where Jude must've kept her clothes.

Jude interrupted my thoughts, "I need to stay at the Academy for another few days before I can leave. I can tell you how to find the Oracle and you and Lucas can go to get your ring. Then you can return here and we can all work together to formulate a plan to get you out of this mess. Tomorrow morning I am going to go back to Ventus to check on my family but then I must return to resume classes. This is my last week of classes. I will complete my courses just in time for my twenty-eighth birthday. If I don't stay to complete these courses, the last ten years were all for naught," Jude said. She looked to Lucas with a question in her eye, "Lucas, do you think I could-" Before she could finish, Lucas held up two Pegasus feathers, one to get her to Ventus and one to get her back to the Academy in time to complete her courses. "Thank you, Lucas," she said, relieved, dropping her shoulders.

"Ok, so here's what you need to know about finding the Oracle," Jude said, and we set to work.

Chapter 13

I lay on my back, unable to sleep, next to Jude in her bed in the dark. I was running through everything she had told us about finding the Oracle to get my power ring. Jude said its location was mysterious and moved from place to place to evade detection. She said that we would need to camp in the Forest of Demeter and seek it out each day. The location would only reveal itself to a Fae with true intentions in their heart.

There were different ways a Fae could attempt to find the Oracle. Each Fae was born to harness magic from the natural resources of the earth, referred to as elemental affinities. There used to be multiple Oracles but they were hunted and killed, which is why the location changed daily, and now only one remained, the Oracle of Isla.

Isla was believed to be over five hundred years old. Her four sisters had all been hunted and killed because of their unique gifts. They were gifted Psychometry, telepathy, mind reading, and fortune-telling. They were descendants of the god Apollo and everyone sought to harness their power, believing they could gain control of the royal Kingdom of Chaos as a whole. If a Lord of a realm could capture an Oracle then he would know when enemies were coming and their kingdom could attack their enemies without warning. They would be undefeatable.

Since I harnessed the element of air, as a citizen of Aether, Jude told me I could find the Oracle by asking the wind. Then the wind would guide me by the breeze. Legends even said that the breeze would whisper to those who listened. I told them that I had received messages on the wind already.

We knew that the air would be my primary elemental affinity because I was a citizen of Aether, or so we thought, but I told Jude I had also cast fire out of my hands during a life or death situation. She said it was possible that I harnessed the affinity of light as well but it could've just been granted to me at the time, by the gods, out of necessity.

I also told her I felt like I could breathe underwater and that I had taken the form of a mermaid but I had also flown using wings. She had never heard of that happening before and said I should ask the Oracle. Especially since I wasn't from the Kingdom of Pontus.

Jude gave us a brief summary of how each element could lead a Fae to the Oracle of Isla, since we didn't know what all I could do yet. If a Fae harnessed the element of light, they could ask the stars to guide them. If it was during the day, they could use fire to illuminate a path. If they harnessed water, they could ask a stream to guide them or cast a rain cloud into the sky to lead them there. If they harnessed the elemental affinity of earth, they could ask the earth to clear a path to lead them there. The earth could also produce vines or flowers to grow along the way. The Fae just needed to have a pure heart.

There was another elemental affinity that was believed to no longer exist. It was the element of darkness. The Fae that harnessed the element of darkness could use shadows to guide them to the oracle. No one had been known to have harnessed the darkness in fifty years and they were said to have all been killed. It sounded like a scary bedtime story for children to me.

Jude had also mentioned that it was possible for me to be equipped to harness more than one elemental affinity. She said that I should try to speak to each one to see if anything else responded to me. If not, the Oracle would reveal my true nature when I met her. "Speak to them," she said. As if I knew how to do that.

I pondered everything Jude had told me. My mind was buzzing from all the knowledge. Lucas was obviously having no trouble sleeping, confirmed by his snoring from the couch at the front of the room. Jude laid very still next to me, her breathing deep.

I had told Jude I really didn't know how to work my magic. She told me to become one with nature and creation. That sounded easier said than done. She said to speak to the wind and it would obey me if I respected it. She said to use it lovingly, respect the earth, and be grateful for what it gave me. She also told me to be confident. That I was a powerful Fae and that nature wanted to do my bidding because I was a creation of the gods. She also said it took focus and concentration to give nature a clear message it could respond to.

Respect, confidence, focus, got it. I think, maybe. I was unsure, but she said the earth wouldn't listen to me until I accepted my true nature.

The next thing I knew, I was slowly waking up. Lucas was sitting up on the couch and Jude had "turned the lights on," she said. Jude was standing up, fully dressed. "I have to go to check on my family. You should start by Pega-traveling to the Forest of Demeter in the Kingdom of Gaia. She quickly explained that even though we could call on the elements for guidance, there were magical beasts along the way that may be able to help us too.

The Forest of Demeter was known to be a place of revelations. It was on the eastern side of the Kingdom of Gaia and, as history told it, many Fae traveled there for information. Because of this, the forest could also be very dangerous. Due to its allure, those who sought answers there made themselves vulnerable. Corrupted Fae lay traps there to rob the travelers. Creatures of the night hunted there because they knew the travelers were foreign and unfamiliar with the area.

Sounded like an adventure to me. And we didn't have any other ideas, so Lucas and I planned to head there after eating breakfast since it was possibly our last real meal for a while.

"They bring breakfast around every morning and drop it off at the door. Sometimes they knock, sometimes they don't. It should be here any moment, though," Jude said from across the room. I crossed the small room and pulled her into a hug.

I pushed back and looked her in the face, "Please check on Father for me. He should complete his sentence today and had plans to return to Ventus to try to help rebuild and scrounge for survivors." She nodded, confirming she would. I really didn't have to ask her, she had always looked after my father anyways.

Dressed in green pants, a black shirt, and a green jacket, Jude took a deep breath. Her black curly hair was so long it still hit her mid-back even when up in a high ponytail atop her head She pulled her pocket open and took one pegasus feathers out. She shut her pocket and patted it, smiling at Lucas. "Thank you so much for making this quick trip home possible," she said gratefully. She walked over to Lucas and kissed him on the cheek. His eyes widened slightly and he smiled at her.

She held the feather in her right hand while opening her left palm. She looked at me and beamed, "I learned to harness the element of light." Her open palm created a flame and it traveled to the tip of her pointer finger. She held it up to the Pegasus feather and said, "To the remains of my home in Ventus." There was a clap of magic and she blinked out of existence.

Lucas walked to the door and opened it, finding that a tray had been placed on the ground outside of the door. He bent down and picked up the tray and walked to the desk. He set the tray down and lifted the lid. There was a heaping serving of bacon, eggs, toast, pancakes, grits, and fruit on the plate. It was a breakfast fit for a king. I guess that should be expected with the price Jude was paying to stay here. She had told me once how much her educational fees were and it made me audibly gasp.

Lucas and I dug in, splitting each item and being satiated with remnants of food still left on the plate. I stood, taking a deep breath. "Lucas, you're such a good friend to come on this insane journey with me. I am grateful for you," I said, in case we died.

Lucas smiled, pulling a feather out of his Pegasus feather bag. It was time to Pega-travel to the Forest of Demeter. "Do you want to try to cast fire in your hand to light this feather?" Lucas asked.

"Sure, I'll give it a shot," I said, thinking of all the things Jude had told me. Respect nature, be confident in myself, and focus on what I wanted to do. I was grateful for the Earth and all she gave me. I knew I could create a flame, maybe. I wanted a flame to appear in my hand. I opened my eyes. Nothing. Maybe I didn't have the ability to harness light.

Lucas held out his hand and willed a flame to life. "Lucas, you didn't tell me you could harness light!" I exclaimed, so proud of him for being a dual elemental.

"I'm a male of great mystery," he joked. "Grab my arm," he said as he held out his elbow to me. I looped my arm through his and gripped his arm with the palm of my other hand. His muscles were rock solid in my grip. When did that skinny, lanky boy become such a strong, grown-up male?

"The Forest of Demeter," he said confidently. With a clap of magic, we blinked out of view of the Academy of Athena. When we reappeared we were surrounded by green, lush bushes and trees. Now what?

Chapter 14

It was early in the day and Lucas and I stood shoulder to shoulder in a forest, not really sure what to do next. I had borrowed a new outfit from Jude and packed a small bag that I had slung over my back. I wore clean, black stretchy pants and, what Jude called a sports bra, with a cut-off shirt. A large section of my toned stomach was exposed but now that we were in the Kingdom of Gaia the weather was much warmer. I was very busty and Jude had explained that a sports bra would be more suitable for the all-terrain traveling that I would be doing. I could see what she meant, I felt comfortable and well suited for the trip.

Lucas had on a short sleeve t-shirt the color of dark, orangish-yellow. He had on long pants that were dark green and had pockets on the side. He wore black boots similar to mine.

Lucas was a head taller than me but much broader compared to my small frame. He had really filled out over the last several years since school. It was hard to look at him in any way other than as a big brother.

I never had a brother or sister, so I had always felt extremely close to Jude even though she was eight years older than I was. Lucas was only three years older, and I felt like this would be a great bonding experience for us, like a brother and sister trip.

Lucas turned his head to me, "So? Where to Lost Princess?" he said with a coy smile.

"Don't even start with that bullshit, Lucas. Besides, I wouldn't be a princess, I would be a duchess, obviously," I said and then laughed.

"Well, we need to speak to the wind, I guess. Have you ever spoken to the wind?" I asked Lucas, my brows raised.

"Yeah, of course. It's easier than you think. I'll show you. Go stand over there behind that tree so that you can't see me," Lucas pointed to a tree that was a good distance away.

I raised my eyebrows and started walking. I looked at the ground, making sure to step over vines and rocks on the forest floor.

I turned around but I didn't see Lucas. Just then, a whisper only I could hear, caressed my ear, "Look up, Evie."

My gaze slowly traveled up and scanned the tree branches until I saw Lucas standing on a branch in the tree top. "How did you get up there?" I asked, surprised and excited.

"I asked the wind to carry me," he stated like it was an obvious answer. I raised an eyebrow at Lucas and crossed my arms. "Ok, ok, I'll show you," he called out.

Lucas stood utterly still. He stretched his arms out, lifting them slowly, palms up. When his palms were level with his shoulders, he said, "Boreas, God of Wind, let the wind carry me to where I desire." Lucas's feet lifted off the branch and gently planted him on a higher branch in another tree.

"What if I don't remember each individual god's name?" I shouted from the forest floor, cupping my mouth so my voice would travel up to him.

I felt wind swirling around my ear as it gently pressed his message into my ear, "Lucky for you, they don't mind. There are four gods of wind, are you telling me you don't know any of their names?"

"No, I don't," I yelled up to him from the forest floor.

"Just address them as 'gods' in your plea to them. You can also think it in your mind, it doesn't have to be said aloud. Just make sure you are grateful to them," the wind whispered the message Lucas had given into my ear.

I blew out a breath. "Here goes nothing," I said aloud to no one. I stretched my hands out and up; just like Lucas had done. "Dear gods of wind, please carry me to the branch Lucas is on so I can push him off of it," and up I went, slowly, before the wind gently placed me on the branch. I took both arms and shoved Lucas off the branch, knowing he could save himself.

Before he hit the ground, a gentle breeze caught him and slowed his downward motion. He rolled onto his back, hands behind his head, floating just above the ground. He stuck his tongue out at me. "Show off," I whispered.

"I heard that, Evie!" He shouted from the ground. I asked the wind to carry me down. I landed carefully next to him as he moved from floating to a standing position. "How did you hear that, I didn't ask the wind to send it to you?" I asked.

"Once the wind has heard you, it knows your voice. It enters your heart and mind, and it knows your needs and wants. It can read your heart as long as you let it and continue to respect it. It's kind of like a conversation. When you enter a room to speak to someone, you may have to address them at first, but not every time you speak," he said, getting lost in his thoughts. "Think of the elements as your friends, as if they are other Fae. Work with them and let them guide you," Lucas said softly.

It sounded... delightful. I closed my eyes. My hair started to blow back on a gentle breeze. The leaves around me began to lift off the ground and pull together, making a swirling mass of leaves in front of me. I reached out to touch them, and the leaves parted around my hand as if made of water but continued to spin in the cyclone I had created with my mind. Whoa.

"Nature is so good and kind to us, Evie. Remember to be grateful for the power it shares with us," Lucas said so kindly. I looked at Lucas like I never had before. It was so rare for a strong male to have such a pure heart. Lucas was a rare find.

"Ok, so back to the Oracle situation. I have already received my ring," he said while spinning it on his finger. The stone was light blue, like the sky, in the shape of wings. There was a small white stone at the top, where the rings joined. It must represent his shifted form, a Griffon, and his elemental affinity, air.

Which made me think of something. "When you met the Oracle for your ring, did she tell you that you could harness fire? It is not on your ring," I asked.

"The oracle shared with me that I had the choice to learn to harness fire. The gods gave me the element of air, but they gave me a choice to accept the element of light into my heart. Of course, I was happy to work to achieve it, but it doesn't answer as clearly to me as air," he said. He leaned in and said conspiratorially, "In my opinion, air is the best element anyway." He winked at me, and I smiled.

It was intriguing to learn more about elemental power. I hadn't really paid much attention growing up because there was a chance I wouldn't receive power at all. I figured since my father was half-mortal, and I didn't know too much about my mother's line, there was a high likelihood that I would be powerless. I didn't want to learn a lot just to be let down by lacking power. Of course, some Fae chose to study and reignite the power that lay dormant in their veins, but I had left it to the gods. I wasn't going to work for something I wasn't destined to have. That was before I knew my life wasn't what I thought. Now I was open to wherever fate and the gods made for me. They were already leading me down a path I couldn't have dreamed up. I wished that I had been better prepared.

"Since I already have my ring, I think you will have to call to the Oracle," Lucas finished his thought from a moment ago.

"Ok, so should I, uh, just ask the wind to take me to the Oracle or...?" I stuttered through my question.

"Sort of. Ask the gods to use the wind to reveal the path to the Oracle to you and your handsome friend," he said, smiling.

I barked a laugh. "Oh my friend thinks he's handsome, does he?" I asked. I bumped my hip into him casually. He looked at me from the corner of his eye, the smile still on his face.

"Ok," I said, taking a deep breath. "Gods of the Wind,-" I started.

Lucas cut me off, "Do you want to know their names, in case it comes up in conversation?"

"Seriously?" I said and then laughed.

"Boreas, God of the North Wind. Zephyrus, God of the West Wind. Notus, God of the South Wind. And Eurus, God of the East Wind," He said proudly.

"Ok, thank you for the history lesson. I will memorize that later," I blew out another breath, smiling. I closed my eyes and held up my hands and said, "Gods of the wind, please use the wind to guide me-"

"And your handsome friend," Lucas interjected again.

"Lucas, would you shut the hell up?" I asked, barking a laugh. "Shut up, so I can think." I raised my arms again and closed my eyes in concentration. "Gods of the air, please use the wind to guide me to the Oracle," I said, squeezing my eyes shut. I slowly opened one eye, peeking out, to see that nothing was happening. I opened both eyes and dropped my arms down to my sides.

"I guess the Gods favor me because, at least, I know their names," he said, smiling, and lightly shoved me.

"Or maybe I couldn't concentrate because you never shut up," I said, crossing my arms. I raised my eyebrows and smirked.

Lucas turned to me and lunged, attempting to tackle me to the ground. The air caught me as I tipped backward and slowly lowered me to the ground. Being best friends with the wind was the coolest. Lucas was laying on top of me when we finally made contact with the grass and he rolled off onto the ground next to me. We laid on our backs, laughing lightly, next to each other for a few moments before I shot up into a sitting position.

I had heard something off in the distance but it was faint. I had to listen carefully.

"What?" Lucas asked, darting up.

"Shut up," I said quickly. I was straining my ears to hear.

"Evie, you need to move. Declan is approaching," the message was delivered to my ear on the breeze.

I asked Lucas, "Did you hear that?"

"Hear what?' he asked, confused.

"That voice! It told me we needed to move, that my kidnapper is approaching. You didn't hear it?" I asked, spinning to search Lucas' face.

"No, I didn't hear it. So should we go, or do you want to keep sitting here asking if I heard it?" Lucas asked, pushing himself into a standing position. He stepped in front of me and reached down with both hands to help me into a standing position. When I stood, we were chest to chest and I looked up into his face. "Where do we go?" I asked, at a loss for ideas.

"We can ask the wind to carry us to another place in the forest, if we can tell it a direction. We can try and fly out of here but it would be hard to break the tree line," he said thinking aloud. "Or we can Pega-travel," he said, looking to me to make a choice.

"Can we Pega-travel to somewhere we've never been? How specific do we have to be?" I asked, not quite sure how it worked.

"I can just ask to go to the North side of the Forest of Demeter and we can start there. We really don't know what area of the forest we are in currently since we were vague in our initial request. Once we search the north area, we can be more specific when we travel," he suggested.

I heard voices off in the distance and grabbed Lucas by the arm. We crouched behind a nearby tree, my eyes darting around the forest looking for Declan. What were the chances that he had found me here?

Then, I saw him. A male I thought was helping me but had so easily manipulated me using his siren gifts. He fed off of my lust and used me. I could kill him. I wasn't sure I was ready to go head to head with him yet though.

Then behind him was Jake, the male that had spared me. I was still so confused about Jake. He was always staring at me and looking after me. When I was near him, lightning filled me. I don't know what I had seen in Declan before. Jake was way more attractive than Declan anyway. He was taller, more muscular, and didn't go around acting like an asshole. He had an undeniable allure. His features were stern-looking but his green eyes had a softness to them when he had shown mercy on me. I wished I could talk to him separately from Declan.

Lucas was now holding the Pegasus feather in one hand and had a small flame over his pointer finger, ready to travel. "Evie, grab my arm," he whispered.

"Hold on, I want to hear what they're saying," I whispered to Lucas.

Jake spoke loudly saying, "Silas, I don't see them."

Declan turned around and said, "I spoke to the light. The flame pointed me in this direction. They are here somewhere." I know the light didn't think that asshole had a pure heart.

Why was he calling Declan 'Silas' and why was Declan using the element of light over his dominant element of water? If Declan was the Lord of Pontus' son, a citizen of the Water Realm, why would he be using fire to guide him? I gasped as realization washed over me. I remembered what Jake said to me outside of the prison, "He's not the Duke."

My gasp drew some unwanted attention. Declan, or Silas, or whatever the fuck his name was, swiveled our way. I grabbed the crook of Lucas' elbow and he touched his flame to the feather. With the feather set alight he whispered, barely audible, "North side of the Forest of Demeter." Before the clap of magic, I saw Declan's mouth form a circle. I could only imagine that he was yelling the word no.

As my feet hit the ground on the north side of the forest, I smiled knowing we had escaped Declan.

Chapter 15

Once we were alone again, I shared my realization with Lucas. Declan was named Silas. Silas had used the element of light multiple times now, instead of water. Was it a coincidence? It was possible that he was a citizen of the Kingdom of Hephaestus, the Realm of Light. Or, was it possible that he had learned to harness the element of light and just liked it?

I also pointed out that someone was helping us. Who tipped us off? Could it be the gods? How was the voice able to always stay a step ahead?

I looked around at the terrain which was slightly different now. The trees here were taller and fuller than where we had been. I could smell the fresh scent from the firs, spruces, and pines around us. It smelled clean and refreshing. The floor was no longer covered in leaves but, instead, was covered in pine needles and pine cones.

It was mid-day now and Lucas and I were getting hungry. Even though Lucas didn't harness the element of earth, he told me I could try and ask the earth for food. I closed my eyes and asked inwardly for a small bush of edible berries. When I opened my eyes nothing appeared. We would need to continue looking for something to eat. Lucas pulled a book out of his pocket called, "How to Tame Magical Beasts: The Friendly Way". He flipped it open.

"What the hell is that?" I asked Lucas, raising an eyebrow.

"You didn't bring any helpful books with you?" Lucas quipped. "Are you even trying?" Lucas said, cracking a smile.

"Where did it come from?" I asked, still surprised.

"I borrowed it from Jude. It was on her desk," Lucas said, returning his attention back to the book.

"You stole it from Jude?" I asked, emphasizing the word stole. I mocked a surprised expression.

"You must've misheard me. I said I borrowed it. Unlike you, I'm going to give it back. Plus, I'm just out here trying to save your ass," Lucas added. My mouth dropped open and slid into a smile.

"You sure are getting snappy lately," I said, not missing his dig. I would never steal from a friend, though. And especially not Jude.

"I think it's the company I keep," he said. I punched him in the arm and smiled.

"Well, anything useful?" I asked, looking over his shoulder at the book.

"There is a lot of information about different magical beasts that we may encounter and what they're capable of," Lucas said. "And how we can combat them," he added.

"So when we see one, are you going to ask it to hold on so we can look it up in the book before it eats us?" I asked sarcastically.

"No, I will turn to you and ask you for help since you possess all the answers," he said back, equally sarcastic. I laughed, enjoying the interaction. "The beasts are categorized by region. Luckily for us, there is information on beasts that have been found to inhabit the Forest of Demeter," he added.

"Thrilling. Where will we sleep? Any ideas?" I asked Lucas, not facing him as I scanned the area.

"We could Pega-travel back to the Academy but we don't want to waste all of the feathers we have. We could find a cave and sleep in it, or you could try and create one, I guess. I actually know a couple of spells for protection, I've just never used them before," Lucas said, thinking aloud again.

"That sounds safe," I mumbled and rolled my eyes.

"Oh ok, let's hear your ideas then," Lucas said, mock sounding mad. I loved the banter and he was being a good sport.

"You are the one who is magically trained, not me," I said as if that was an excuse.

He laughed. "So are you saying I am wiser or..." he trailed off.

"No, I am saying, I have high expectations for you and you're not meeting them," I said with a fake pouty face. He burst out a laugh. "Maybe your loud ass laugh is how they found us," I quipped.

"You are quite rude," Lucas said, so proper.

I rolled my eyes. "Ok, here's an idea, oh wise one. Let's start off by trying to stay out here and if it's not working or we're in danger, we will Pega-travel somewhere safer," I offered as a suggestion.

"Sounds good to me, Athena," he said, taunting me.

"I'd like to think if I had been a goddess, I would have been Athena, Goddess of Wisdom. Thank you very much for acknowledging that," I said, smugly.

"Oh look at you. You knew the name of a goddess," he said mockingly, starting to clap. He threw a fake, impressed look on his face.

"You are funny," I said, walking up to him and shoving him. Instead, my hands crashed into his hard muscles and I was moved backward, having the opposite effect of what I had intended.

"For a Duchess, you aren't very strong," he teased. My mouth dropped open.

I raised my hands and willed the wind to knock him over. He blasted backward and hit a tree. Both of my hands flew over my mouth in horror. I ran to where he had fallen. "Are you alright?" I asked, scared. He started laughing like I had never hit him or maybe he was impressed. "You asshole," I said, wanting to punch him. I leaned over him, picked up a bunch of pine straw, and threw it in his face. I laughed loudly and stood back up. Lucas lay there defenseless.

I reached my hand out to help him up. "Seriously?" he asked.

"Yeah, seriously, asshole, give me your hand. I'm trying to help your dumb ass," I said.

He reached up and I swatted his hand away and spun on my heel. He started laughing again. "Get over here and help me up," he called after me.

With a huff and a loud, dramatic sigh, I turned around and offered my hand again. He grabbed it, yanked me down to lay down next to him, grabbed a handful of pine straw, and threw it in my face. We laughed. Who knew I was supposedly a duchess and was being hunted?

We lay there for a few minutes before either of us spoke again. I still had a smile on my face when he let out a sigh and said, "We should scope out a place to sleep before nightfall. Then we can practice casting magic until it's time to sleep. We could even sleep in shifts if you're worried."

"Well, since we are on the north side, maybe we could exit the forest and see what lay beyond it," I said, sitting up with a shrug. I turned to face him. He was still lying on the ground and stretched his arms up over his head and placed his palms face up, under his head. His biceps were huge and were stretching the sleeves of his shirt. His dark brown eyes were glistening.

"Do you want to try flying?" he said with a smirk. "Since we are not in a hurry, we can find a clearing to take off in," he added.

I sat up quickly and looked back at him. "The only time I have flown was when I feared for my life. I am not sure I remember what I did to summon wings, but I do want to practice," I said, excitement rising in me.

We decided to find a spot to fly out of. The trees were thinner here, and the ground was drier and harder. It might be easier to take off out of here. We walked until we found a clear area from which Lucas was sure we could take off. We walked to the center of the clearing and Lucas said, "Ok, shift into your form."

"Well, that's the thing. I had wings when I shifted, but my body was the same. I even spent some time underwater as a mermaid. But even when I didn't have a fin, I could still breathe underwater," I said, confused. "I'm not really sure what my 'form' is," I said.

"That's interesting; I have never heard of someone only half shifting or having two forms. The water thing could mean you can harness water, so it was just moving away from your mouth as you willed it," he said, thinking aloud as usual. "Are you sure you saw wings? Because maybe you were using your ability to harness air and were riding on the breeze and just didn't know it?" he asked.

"I definitely saw wings. They were huge, and they were white," I said remembering.

"Well, concentrate and see if you can bring them out again, if not, you can ride me," he said.

"You wish," I replied quickly.

He scoffed and his mouth dropped open. I laughed. "You are so inappropriate for a duchess," he said, throwing in an insult of his own.

"I'm not a duchess. That's just what some no-name maniac said," I said, lightheartedly. He looked at me and cocked his head with his hands on his hips. "Just shut up so I can concentrate," I said.

I blew out a breath, trying to will my wings to come out again. Nothing. I outstretched my arms to see if that changed anything. Nothing. It was frustrating.

"I think you're getting frustrated too quickly and shutting down like you don't have enough confidence," he said.

"Shut up, bird beak. I'm plenty confident. Just let me ride you this time," I said, rolling my eyes. Maybe if I could practice alone, I could do it. I loved being with Lucas, but I had always been kind of on my own with my charming personality.

"If I let you ride me this time, you won't be able to quit," He said, thrusting his hips into an imaginary person in front of him. I barked a laugh.

"Oh, look who's inappropriate now," I said, loving it. I got along with very few people, but I had to admit I enjoyed Lucas' personality.

He quickly shifted into his griffon form right before my eyes. He stood as tall as a Fae, with long white feathers covering his head. The feathers faded into dark brown past his neck and onto his shoulders. He had a sharp, pointed beak and large brown eyes. His head jerked around quickly, mimicking the motions of an eagle. He looked like a giant eagle from the midsection up. His wings were folded up, but I could tell they were significant. His arms were now more like front legs with large eagle feet with sharp talons. The lower half of his body was that of a lion with strong, lean muscles and short tan fur. He had a long tail like that of a lion. Due to shifting, he was standing on his hind legs but dropped onto all fours. His head still came up to my shoulders. He was a remarkable beast.

He lowered a wing so I could climb on. I reached up and grabbed his long feathers between his wings and used my upper body strength to hoist myself up. He took off before I was situated, flapping his wings and running through the clearing. I almost tumbled off but he would've gotten too much pleasure out of that. "Idiot," I whispered to the wind. Lucas cawed so I knew the wind had delivered the message to his ear, wherever an eagle's ear was. I threw my leg over his back and squeezed my knees together to remain upright. His wings beat against my legs as he flapped harder and harder, lifting us off the ground.

We raced up into the sky until we were high enough to look off into the distance in all directions. We leveled out and glided along smoothly. I gripped his brown feathers, as his wings beat in front of my legs. I was squeezing my legs around him just like I had when I had ridden Lenore. I missed her. I hoped I could locate her again someday.

We flew for quite a long time. The endless trees were beautiful except it wasn't what we needed at this time. The sun was low in the sky now and we needed to find a place to sleep. Finally, just past the trees, I saw some rocky cliffs that I wanted to look into. I spoke onto the breeze, "There, up ahead to the right, there are cliffs."

Lucas cawed in response once the message was delivered. He began to lower us until we neared the ground. He lowered his large, bird feet to grab at the ground to steady us. With a couple of hops and backward flaps of his wings, we landed. His strong, lion legs landed with a thump. I climbed down and Lucas knocked me in the ass with his wing. "Asshole," I whispered into the wind and he cawed in response once the wind delivered the message to him.

I looked at the cliffs, which acted as an overhang for the area below, making it the perfect place to sleep. It wasn't a cave with an unknown end, possibly housing monsters which was comforting. But it also served as protection from any weather and would keep us hidden. I turned to Lucas, finding that he was shifted back into his Fae form, and said, "I think this is perfect." Lucas smiled in agreement.

"I'm going to start going over some protection spells. I should be able to make us camouflaged into the rock," he said, holding up his hands. He closed his eyes and I could see magic leaving his hands. White tendrils flowed from his hands like I had seen the night I had been with Declan but his magic had been red. Lucas' white tendrils spun around me and then him. My skin started to glimmer everywhere like I was sparkling. I looked up at Lucas and his skin did the same. Then I could no longer see him.

I panicked. "Lucas?" I said nervously.

I felt something reach out and touch my arm. "I'm still here, Evie. No one can see us, but if we keep physical contact we won't lose each other," he said, relief washing over me.

"Oh for a second I thought you had messed up the spell and I would never have to hear you squawk again," I said, not meaning it.

He laughed, "You are such a bitch."

I laughed. I had never heard him say bitch in our whole lives. "I am really bringing out the worst in you," I said.

He laughed too. He draped his arm over my shoulder. "What now?" I asked. I couldn't see his face, so I wasn't getting as good of a read on him.

"If you're tired, we could lay down, and try and get some rest," he said. It was good that we had started looking for a place to sleep so early in the day because it had taken so long. Plus the journey had made me exhausted. He lifted his arm off of my shoulder. "Where did you go?" I asked, nervously.

He handed me something. "Here, I took my shirt off for you to lay on. We will have to lay on the ground but I can use the air as a blanket to keep us warm," he said, softly.

"That's awfully kind of you, bird brain," I said. I put the shirt down on the cave floor and smoothed it out with my hands. I tried to locate it and lay on it. He reached down to find out where I was, his hand on my arm. He crawled in behind me and laid up against my back.

"I'm just trying to keep us warm. Not trying to make this weirder than it needs to be," he said. I burst out laughing. It was comforting to have Lucas here. I wasn't sure how I would ever repay him for this. Maybe if I was some kind of duchess, I could gift him my wealth. I certainly didn't care about it and he was the type that would do something beneficial with it.

It was good to know that he felt the same way I did. We were just friends and that's how it would stay.

Chapter 16

I snapped awake but it wasn't morning. It took a few moments for everything to settle in my mind. I had a nightmare that I was lost and alone. In the dream, I wandered through a forest in a torn purple robe. I had something in my hand but I didn't know what it was. I was lost and scared.

My mind settled and I realized I was in a cave, in the Forest of Demeter, with my invisible friend but I was safe, relatively speaking. I calmed. The breeze started to speak to me. I remained still so I could listen.

"Declan's name is actually Silas. He knows you seek the Oracle for your power ring. He will be hot on your trail. When the sun rises, move south," the wind whispered in my ear. The wind had a voice though, that I almost recognized but I wasn't sure where I had heard it before. I mulled it over for a few minutes, figuring it would be hard to get back to sleep. Lucas had mentioned that these messages could be a trap but I had never really considered it. I didn't know why but I trusted the voice.

As I continued to lay there, considering who could be sending me these messages, something caught my eye. Outside of the cave, I saw a glowing figure. It was like a wolf but it had wisps of blue all over it and trailing behind it. I wasn't actually sure if it was a solid figure or made entirely of the blue and white wisps. It looked serene and delicate, not like a typical wolf. I sat up and watched it move about the trees near our cave. It crossed the path, sniffing around the trees, and two more glowing, wispy wolves walked out after it. They were much smaller and looked as though they were the larger wolf creature's pups. I smiled as

I watched them walk to the next tree, sniffing about. They were getting closer to the cave entrance but I felt confident that they couldn't see us. Had it not been for Lucas' concealment spell, I figured they would've run off by now. Or attacked us.

I heard a scratching noise come from, what sounded like, above the cave. The wispy wolf creatures whipped their attention to the area above the cave and, before their eyes could even widen, a green blur launched at them.

The green beast hit the ground hard, taking the biggest wolf creature down with it. The beast looked like a green dragon but with the legs of a dog. Its tail tapered off like a worm instead of spikes like a dragon. Its jaws snapped with long, pointed teeth and its tongue was like that of a snake. It had four spikes on its head where eyes should be. The spikes moved around as if they were antennae directing its path.

The wolf creature cried out in a loud moan. The beast took a bite out of the wolf creature's neck and blue blood began to spew. My hands flew to my mouth as I watched in horror not knowing what to do. I turned to see if Lucas was awake but he was still invisible. I was afraid to speak. I didn't know how well their hearing was. The blue wolf yelped. The color of its blue wisps began to turn green and then yellow. Then red and orange were added, making it look like a fire. The green beast on top began to shriek as the fire began to burn its paws. It did not have wings like a dragon and could not easily escape. It jumped off of the flaming wolf but the fire shot after it. Soon, the green beast was engulfed in flame and shrieks filled the night air.

Smoke traveled up into the sky until the green beast was no more. The fire died down until it turned back into the blue wispy wolf. Its pups came bouncing out of the woods, floating on the air. The mother wolf ran to both of them, licking them on the head. Then they resumed their hunt as if nothing had happened.

I was breathing heavily but I hadn't said a word because I didn't want to be detected. Lucas' hand slid up my arm gently, as if to avoid scaring me, but I jumped anyway.

"Did you see that?" I whispered.

"Yes, I was afraid to draw their attention, so I didn't say anything," Lucas whispered back.

"Good job not being an idiot for once," I said, trying to break the tension but still terrified.

After several long moments, I laid back down. I didn't get back to sleep until Lucas had slung his arm over my arm. I took a deep breath and tried to focus. When I was younger, sometimes my father wouldn't return until after I was asleep. Jude would often come over, but when she wasn't there, she taught me how to comfort myself. I would focus on the life I hoped to have someday. I started thinking about a day when I could walk around freely without being chased. I could spend time with my father and remember this crazy adventure I went on with Lucas. I smiled and drifted back off to sleep.

When I awoke again it was light out. I rolled over and didn't see Lucas so I reached out to feel for him and accidentally jammed my fingers into his eye.

"Ow!" he exclaimed. "What was that for?" he asked like I did it on purpose.

"I can't see you. How the fuck could I have possibly jabbed you in the eye on purpose?" I asked

Suddenly we were both visible, lying on the ground facing each other. Lucas rubbed his eyes. I had forgotten he was shirtless. He was impressively muscular compared to the last time I had seen him.

"Lucas, the wind spoke to me in the night before the beast attack," I said. His eyes widened and he raised himself into a sitting position.

"What did it say?" he asked. I told him what the wind said to me, confirming what I had already kind of figured out and adding that we needed to head south today.

We got up and Lucas threw his shirt back on. We both stepped out of the cave. I concentrated, asking the earth if it could spare some corn for us. That must've been the right way to ask because when I opened my eyes there were heaps of corn in front of me. Lucas' eyes widened. "Great job, Evie," he said proudly. We walked down to a stream that I had spotted at the bottom of the cliffs. We washed our hands and faces and drank some water.

"Pega-travel?" Lucas asked.

"Pega-travel," I confirmed. He reached in his pocket for the Pegasus feathers and took one out.

"Ready?" he asked, offering his elbow.

He opened his palm to cast the fire, "Let me," I said. I closed my eyes and released a long steady breath. I held my palm upwards and internally asked the god of light to please cast a flame in my hand. Now that I knew I had harnessed the element of light before, I was confident I could do it again. I opened my eyes, and a flame danced in my palm. My mouth opened in surprise, then faded to a smile.

Lucas beamed with pride. "You're really starting to pick this up, Evie," he said, smiling softly. I smiled in response. It was nice to have his encouragement and know he would call me on my bull shit when I needed him to. I touched the flame to the feather. "South side of the Forest of Demeter," he said.

With a clap of magic, we appeared in a different part of the forest. The trees were more like they had been the day before. The ground was scattered with twigs and leaves. The trees looked like oaks and redbuds. It felt sunnier here and more humid. The ground was softer and damper underneath the leaves.

Since I had struck a bit of luck lately, I lifted my hands, palms up. I internally asked the gods of wind and light to guide me to the oracle. Now that I knew I could harness light too, more doors were opened for me. I opened my eyes. Nothing, again. I sighed.

"It could be that we're just not in the right place or aren't close enough," Lucas said, trying to be optimistic.

"Let's spend the day, casting magic then," I said. I still had a lot to learn and needed to practice.

Lucas walked me through a couple of simple things. He showed me how to cast a light overhead so that I could see when it was dark. He showed me how to capture air and bend it around things. He explained that air was his strongest element because he was a citizen of the Kingdom of Aether. He had the choice to accept light as an element he could harness, but it would never be as strong as his ability to harness air. He said he also tried to study how to harness water and earth but it just never clicked into place for him. He told me about others' magic that he had witnessed and how different Fae could harness the elements differently. Basically, the opportunities were endless if you had a good relationship with nature. He said it was important to let nature guide me and not struggle against it. I felt like any use of the elements was a gift and I was glad to experience it. He also told me he thanked the gods internally after he used his gifts.

I started practicing. I cast balls of light and fire in my hands. I cast them at nearby trees. I felt very in tune with air, but I did want to further my knowledge. I practiced using air to manipulate objects around me. I willed the air to delicately pick up rocks and leaves from the forest floor and carry them to me. I had used earth magic before for food, but I wasn't sure about the extent of my abilities to work with the element. Lucas had explained that sometimes a Fae could dip into an element without actually harnessing it, but we had hope. I felt pretty confident that air and light called to me easily and that I would at least be a dual elemental. I still couldn't pinpoint what my shifted form was.

Lucas sat and flipped open the book he had taken from Jude's room as I practiced. We spent all of the morning practicing and discussing different beasts in the forest. By lunch, Lucas said, "You should rest. You probably feel like your magic has depleted."

"What would that feel like?" I asked, honestly.

"You would feel tired or like you have become ill. You would feel like your body is dragging and empty," he added.

"I feel fine," I said, with a shrug.

"That's odd. It's ok to tell me you're tired. Even for a badass duchess such as yourself, without your power ring to replenish your magic, you will get tired quickly. It's normal, don't worry," he said.

"Let me try to find the Oracle again," I said, ignoring him. I held my hand up and asked the gods to guide me. Nothing. I blew out a long breath, annoyed.

"I could try," Lucas said, holding up his hands and closing his eyes. I waited and watched. Suddenly the wind changed and we were being guided forward by the breeze. He opened his eyes. "I guess even Fae who have their power ring can still track the Oracle," he said.

"That's not good. That means dipshit can still track it, meaning he can track me because he knows that's where I'm headed," I said. Lucas laughed, no longer surprised at my foul language. I had kind of hoped Fae, with their power rings, couldn't track the Oracle anymore because then Declan wouldn't know where I was heading.

The wind encouraged us along. Judging by the sun, we were

heading north. Since we had been on the south side of the forest, I assumed we were now traveling deep into the forest. We walked along, guided by the wind, not speaking much. The breeze was all around us. If we had tried to speak, we would've had to yell over the soft hum of the wind.

It felt good on my skin, like a hug from the earth. I had always loved the breeze, as if it had always called to me. As a child of the Kingdom of Aether, I hoped to be able to harness the power of air. It was such a delicate element, yet could quickly become violent. It was not always seen and appreciated but always there. It was stealthy and humble. I was grateful for the air. The air brushed my hair back over my shoulder and I wanted to lean into it.

As we walked, we stepped up and down over rocks. We had to walk around trees, over vines, and through the leaves. The leaves rustled overhead and occasionally dropped to the forest floor. We could hear sounds of distant birds and squirrels running about playing and hunting.

We walked along for a while, not speaking, just enjoying the forest and the breeze. My muscles strained after a while from the constant up and down. I stubbed my toe on a rock and flew forward. Lucas caught me from around my arm and steadied me. "I think we should rest and look for something to eat," I said.

Lucas reached into his pocket and grabbed two pieces of toast, handing me one. "Where the hell did you get toast?" I asked, smiling wide.

"It was from breakfast yesterday. I stuffed some in my pocket, knowing we would be hungry today after just eating berries. That was before I knew you could harness earth. It took great restraint not to eat both pieces when you couldn't see me last night," he said, smiling. He took a bite, "I used the concealment spell to hide it from myself as well." Sitting on the forest floor, he took a bite of toast. I looked down at my flimsy piece of bread and started eating it as well, taking a seat next to him. Lucas was incredibly thoughtful.

Once I finished eating, I sighed and said, "Alright, let's go then." I stood and turned to Lucas, who was still sitting. I offered my hand to help him up.

"Oh, have you not learned your lesson yet?" he said smiling, grabbing my hand and squeezing it.

"Lucas, get the fuck up," I said, rolling my eyes and smiling.

"Such a bitch," he said, standing. He was still gripping my hand but didn't use it to pull himself up. He pulled me into a tight hug. I rested my face against his chest and looped my arms around his back. His arms wrapped around me over my shoulders.

I felt so safe in his arms. I felt protected by his strength. I appreciated his guidance and his help. For someone to drop everything they had going on, at a moment's notice, really meant a lot to me. Lucas was warm and thoughtful.

He pulled away from the hug, as if he felt the same. He didn't try to take things further, making me feel comfortable having these moments with him. If I thought he had feelings for me, I would be worried about being so close to him, fearing that I would confuse him. As it were, things were pretty perfect between us.

As we drew back from the hug, an arrow zoomed between us. My head snapped in the direction of where it came from. Declan, or Silas, was running at us, a bow slung around his back. Where the fuck did he get a bow and arrow?

"Where the fuck did he get a bow and arrow?" I just had to say aloud. The arrow barely missed us as we had just released our hug and pulled away from each other.

Behind Silas, several males were running in our direction, each with various weapons. Silas's male to the right had a club in one hand and was waving it over his head. Three more male had swords drawn. Jake was walking calmly while everyone else ran. Weren't there more of them than that?

I whipped my head around to see three males approaching from the side directly opposite of Silas. Lucas pushed me away. "Run," he said, with fear in his eyes. He held his hands up, palms pointing at Silas, and willed a strong gust of air that knocked all of them on their asses.

It was too late. A male grabbed my arm, and I jerked it back quickly, making contact with his face using my elbow. He grabbed his face and leaned forward. I pushed the back of his head down as I drew my knee up and kneed him right in the face. He fell backward, and I spun, finding another male approaching me. As I spun, I used the motion to kick him in the face. The kick knocked him backward off his feet. He turned onto his side and tried scrambling up as the third male reached for me. I reared back and landed a punch square in the nose, knocking him out cold. The second male was now back on his feet, and I readied my fighting stance. He swung his fist, and I blocked it with my left forearm, using the distraction to land an upper hook with my right. His head jerked backward, and I swept his feet out from under him, knocking him on his ass. I took a quick look around and saw Lucas fist fighting with Silas. Silas had a bloody lip, and Lucas had the upper hand, but he was overtaken by two other guards approaching with magic binding gloves. Jake stood watching the exchange, and I moved towards them. A strong gust of wind pushed me backward.

"Turn and run," the wind whispered in my ear. I fought against the breeze, but it pushed against me until it forced me to take several steps backward. I went against the wind until I was swept off my feet and carried away by the breeze. Jake was now looking at me with a smirk on his face. I had to get to Lucas, but it seemed impossible. The wind carried me away from the group, and I watched them disappear into the distance.

I didn't want to get too far from Lucas or lose the way, so I watched as I was lifted away in the direction we had been. Now I wished I had some Pegasus feathers in my pocket. Lucas and I should've known this was a possibility. I should've carried Pegasus feathers too. We should've talked about a rendezvous plan. I can't believe I was so stupid to think we could have just walked up to the Oracle without any challenges and been handed my ring.

What in hades, hell, and purgatory was I thinking? Eventually, the breeze set me down lightly, like a mother would a child, and I took off back in the direction I had come from. I ran and ran and ran. I stopped only when I realized everything was too quiet, and I was heavily panting. I hid behind a tree and peeked to see if I was being followed. I leaned my back against the tree, my hands bracing me on either side to keep me upright.

Now, I was all alone in the Forest of Demeter. I barely had any control over my magic and no Pegasus feathers. The sun was descending in the sky now, and the daylight was slipping away. Ok, I needed to pull myself together. I had been taking care of myself for a long time. Just because I had help for the last few days didn't mean I was incapable of being alone now.

In the distance, I heard the howl of a wolf. Oh good, a wolf. Or better yet, a werewolf. I started looking around, trying to get my bearings. The moon illuminated the sky enough that I could see the trees nearest to me. I could hear the rustling of leaves and the movement of animals. I heard birds in the distance chirping as if the forest never slept. I wanted to creep quietly through the woods but wasn't sure how. My steps seemed louder than usual in the stillness around me.

I ducked under low-lying branches and watched my footing. I heard a sudden crash like something had fallen out of a tree, and I froze. I tried to become in tune with nature to understand what was approaching me. I could hear footsteps and what sounded like something being drug across the ground. Leaves crunched as the creature got closer to where I was standing. I was somewhat hidden by the tree nearest to me, depending on what direction the thing came from. It started getting closer and crossed into the area illuminated by the moonlight, and my eyes widened.

Out walked a huge lizard-like animal, almost the size of a male Fae. It crawled on all four of its short legs, its tail dragging behind. Its tongue kept darting out of its mouth like a snake's. It was creeping along, hunting me. I looked up into the tree and decided to use air magic to carry myself onto a limb. I held my palms out, pointing them at the ground, and sent a silent plea to the gods. I needed to move slowly so that it wouldn't hear me.

I started lifting off the ground slowly. The moment my feet left the ground, the beast shot across the forest floor and launched itself at my leg. I raised my palm, shooting fire out of my hand instinctively. The beast screamed, drawing way too much attention to us. It fell to the ground and shot away in the opposite direction, still ablaze from my fire. I was panting and my mind was reeling. I needed to move from this spot before other creatures decided to show up to see what the commotion was.

As I took a step, pain shot through my leg. I looked down, still panting. There was a green, glowing substance on my leg and a tear in my pants. I knelt down, pulling my pants back to see four puncture marks on my leg. I sucked in a breath. I really needed Lucas and his stupid book right now. I also needed to go. Maybe I could carry myself on the wind. My leg was starting to burn now as the adrenaline wore off.

A breeze rustled the leaves and made its way around my body up to my ear. "Silas has your friend," the breeze caressed my ear. "Ask the breeze to take you to him. I will help you," the male voice said.

"Who are you?" I asked, sending it back on the breeze. I sucked in a breath and my voice was laced with pain.

The breeze carried another message to me, "Sana is a healing spell." It sounded like a soft, far away whisper.

"Who are you?" I said, with more urgency. No answer came. Clutching my leg, I could feel sweat starting to bead on my forehead. My entire leg was on fire. I kept my hands where they were on my leg and breathed, "Sana." After a moment, I could feel the pain receding and drawing back towards the punctures. The punctures illuminated green and disappeared. My mouth dropped open.

Spells were a more complicated form of magic. A Fae had to be quite powerful for certain spells. Some weaker Fae could do simple spells. I thanked the gods for allowing me to borrow their magical gifts because I knew I wasn't powerful enough.

After a few moments of being thankful, I remembered I was sitting on the ground in the Forest of Demeter, by myself, in the middle of the night. I needed to turn back and go the way I came. I had stopped panting, feeling restored, and readied myself to run. But I was so thirsty. Maybe I could call on the water.

I held my hands out in front of me like a bowl. I closed my eyes and asked the gods, "Please, god of water, fill my hands with water that I may drink." I opened my eyes and watched my hands fill with clean, cool water. My mouth dropped open. I was so proud of myself and shocked. Now I knew I could harness the elemental affinities of water, light, earth, and air. This was incredible. While I began to think about how my father could only harness air, it seemed impossible that I had all four elemental affinities. An uncomfortable knot in my stomach reminded me that he wasn't my birth father and that I didn't really know what I was capable of. Maybe I was just dipping into other elements, and not actually harnessing them. I had so many questions still.

Suddenly, I heard a noise approaching. I asked the wind to carry me up into the tree I was standing at the foot of. The wind picked me up and cradled me, lifting me up the tree trunk until it gently placed me down on a high branch. The noise was coming right toward me and was growing increasingly loud. Panic was rising in my chest.

I wondered if I could will my wings out again. Then I saw her weaving through the trees before I closed my eyes to try. A black figure headed my way with four legs, still saddled and ready to ride.

"Lenore!" I cried in shock. She approached the foot of the tree I was in and bowed her head. The wind carried me down to her before I could even ask. I hugged Lenore's neck tightly. How had she found me? She was so loyal and I loved her for that. Had the gods sent her back to me? I thanked them anyway. I continued to pet her and offered her water from my hands. She lapped it up. When she finished drinking, I hugged her again and she nudged me with her nose. I filled my hands with berries and she slurped them up too. I pet her neck, looking into her eyes. I smiled at her and then jumped into the saddle.

I didn't have much time if I wanted to try and catch up to Lucas. I guided her towards the way I had come. I wouldn't be able to run her hard through this forest in the dark. The terrain was uneven, and there were low-hanging branches. I figured she could still travel faster than I would be able to on foot.

I didn't think it was possible for me to harness a fourth element, but I was going to ask the earth to guide me so that it would make an easier path for Lenore to travel on. As Lenore stomped through the rugged terrain, I held her reins in one hand and lifted my other hand, palm facing out. I knew the name of the goddess of the earth because there was a whole kingdom named after her. I closed my eyes and asked, "Gaia, goddess of earth, please provide me with a path to my friend Lucas."

I opened my eyes to see a path clearing ahead, trailing into darkness. The path was smooth and void of rocks. It wound through the trees and was made of soft, brown dirt. I kicked Lenore on each side, hopping up to sit high in her saddle. She took off down the path, and I internally thanked the gods.

I wasn't sure if I could truly harness all four elements or not but I was happy for whatever I could do. I was so grateful for what the gods had granted me so far. The sky's stars brightened and sparkled as if they were congratulating me.

Chapter 17

It was pitch black out now. I had internally asked for an orb of light, and it had come to fruition out in front of Lenore. The light was cast off her, facing forward as if it were beaming through her eyes. She trotted, no longer at a run. We had traveled for a long while. I held out my hand, palm up as Lenore cantered below me. I thought of a handful of berries and opened my eyes to see that the gods had granted it. I ate a handful while pulling the reins up to stop Lenore. I slung my leg over and jumped down. As I approached her head, I ran my hand along her black, sleek body. She turned slightly, blowing out a breath from her nose. I held out my hand, and she slurped up the berries again. She had worked up an appetite traveling through the night. There was always time to stop and have a snack. Lucas would understand.

I willed more berries into my hand again and again until she was no longer interested. I turned to look at the path. On one side, I stretched my hand out, palm facing down. I willed a small pool of fresh, clean water onto the ground. I walked over, cupped the water in my hands, and pulled it to my mouth to drink it. Then, I stepped aside and pulled Lenore's rein to encourage her to drink. She drank happily, then nudged me on the shoulder with her nose in thanks.

I ran my hand down her face several times and smiled at her. She had a long, black mane that hung over her eyes. Her dark eyes looked so peaceful. I brushed her mane out of her eyes while I smiled at her. She was so beautiful.

I heard a twig snap somewhere off in the darkness. I willed the light to go out and climbed onto Lenore quickly. I urged her forward slowly. A growl cut through the air not far behind us. I kicked Lenore hard, crouching low in the saddle, and we took off. I cast a tiny light, faint enough for us to see. Light. I held the element of light, meaning I could cast fire. Everything was so new I often forgot what I could do.

Gripping the reins tightly, I threw my free hand behind me and willed fire to shoot out behind us. A massive fireball shot out, and flames engulfed the path. Several of the animals squealed in response. Once illuminated, I could see that four wolves were chasing us. The fire engulfed them and the trees lining the path. The fire had presented itself as a much bigger orb than I had intended. I needed to learn how to control my elements to increase my accuracy. But I'd rather have too much than not enough, I supposed. I cast another ball of fire just to ensure they had been killed, and they howled and cried until they went silent.

I slowed Lenore until we were stopped, and I listened. I leaned forward, rubbing my hand down her neck several times before sitting back in the saddle. I urged Lenore forward, but I felt we weren't alone. I squinted my eyes and searched the darkness behind us.

I didn't see anything approaching, so I swung back around. Way up ahead, I could see what looked like embers from a fire. I slowed Lenore to a stop again and jumped off of her back. I stood next to her, petting her neck and staring toward the fire. I squinted, using my Fae sight, and I could see several males lying on the ground. Perhaps this was Silas and his guards. Maybe Lucas was here too.

Lenore snorted loudly, and I startled. "Lenore!" I whispered sharply. They hadn't heard us approach, so maybe they hadn't heard her snort either.

Someone in the camp sat up, looking around. "Well, shit," I

muttered. I whispered on the breeze, "Lucas, I'm here to rescue your dumb ass." I willed the message to travel to him on a breeze. I swore I heard the idiot laugh.

The male that was seated stood. "Ok, well, I am standing right here, ready to be rescued. Duchesses sure are slow at rescuing," he sent back to me on a breeze.

"How do I get you out without being detected?" I asked him in the breeze.
How was I going to approach this camp quietly?

"Carry me out of here on the air. What are you waiting for?" he asked on the wind. I concentrated, and Lucas started floating on a breeze. Why didn't he carry his own ass out?

He floated to the path, then along the way until he reached us. "Did you have a nice nap? I, on the other hand, haven't slept because I have been out here trying to save your ass while you have been laying around sleeping," I whispered but made sure the tone was clipped. I turned, and we headed away from the camp, walking slowly to be quiet.

He laughed at my comment, trying to be quiet. As we crept away from the camp, he held up his hands, showing me his magic binding gloves.

"Oh, you got some fancy new gloves too?" I said.

"Yeah, and some new friends that don't call me an idiot all the time," he said, and I laughed.

"Probably because they don't know you very well yet," I quipped.

"You're insufferable," he replied, and I could hear the smile on his face.

"So, did you girls go on a shopping spree for your new gloves? Is there a matching coat too or...." I trailed off.

"Oh, you're not done yet, then? Here's a question for you then.

Where'd you get a fucking horse?" he asked.

"Oh, this is Lenore. Lenore, this is Lucas," I said as if introducing them. She trotted alongside us as we walked.

After we felt like we were far away from Silas and his cronies, I cleared my throat. "How do we get these gloves off?" I asked seriously.

"Why? Do you want to borrow them? Are you really that jealous?" he asked with a pout.

"No idiot, I thought you might like to cast magic again someday," I spat.

He barked a laugh. "Ok, this can be complicated," he started. "Usually, only the person that put the gloves on can remove them, but there may be another way," he trailed off.

"Who put them on you?" I asked, knowing the answer.

"Your best friend, Silas," he smiled. The sky started to lighten a little. I knew morning was coming, and I hadn't slept yet.

"How were you still able to talk on the breeze?" I asked.

"I was replying to your message, and the wind brought it back to you. Essentially, I wasn't using magic; you were," he said.

A twig snapped, and I turned around to see males rising in the camp. We were a good distance away, but I could see the bodies rising in the darkness around the fire. One cast a ball of light above the camp, confirming they were awake, and they must've realized Lucas was missing.

Clouds started to roll in quickly. They seemed focused on the area where Silas and his guards had been. They collected over their camp, gray and full. The bottoms burst from the clouds, and rain started to pour down on them. Thunder crackled, and lightning struck directly into the center of the camp. I barked a surprised laugh.

"Did you do that?" Lucas asked.

"I wanted it to happen, but I didn't ask per se," I said, raising my eyebrows.

"It happened too quickly for it to be a natural storm. And lightning struck dead center in their camp, so it was probably you," Lucas said, his eyebrows raised now too.

I looked at the area in awe. Had I done that? I hoped Silas burned to death by the lightning; then, I quickly took back the thought. I wasn't sure that I was ready to murder anyone yet. Plus, I wanted to be there to face him and watch him in his misery.

"While I am thinking of it," I said, turning back to Lucas. "We need a plan next time. We should come up with a place to meet if we get separated again. We can travel there by Pegasus feathers," I said.

"Yeah," Lucas nodded. He stopped walking. "Reach in and grab a couple of feathers out of the bag in my pocket. They're camouflaged in this pocket," he said. He jutted his knee towards me and gestured his head to the pocket on his thigh. I reached in and felt the bag but couldn't see it. I took two feathers out, but I didn't have any pockets. I shoved them into my sports bra between my breasts, which were squished down with the "magic" of the sports bra.

I turned my attention back to the gloves. They came up past his wrists and were dark gray. They shimmered with magic and looked beautiful but prevented Lucas from accessing his magic. The gloves looked like a flexible material, but the wearer could not move their fingers at all and had little use of their hands.

"If we can get the gloves off, maybe we could keep them and use them the next time we see that asshole," I said. I rivaled most males with my tenacity. I fought dirty. I wasn't above biting, spitting, hair pulling, or kicking someone where it hurt most. I was also able to knock someone out cold with one hit. A tavern goer, and friend of my father's, had made sure I was equipped to do so.

Lucas stopped walking and turned to face me. "Forest Fairies," he said, grabbing both of my arms just above the elbows, unable to squeeze them through the gloves. I searched his face.

"What?" I paused, thinking for a second. He looked at me excitedly. "Are you waiting on me to use telepathy to understand what you mean, or would you like to just come out and say it? I don't know if you noticed, but we are-" I started.

"Forest fairies," he cut me off. His eyes beamed. "They were in the book that you never thanked me for bringing," he said, smugly. He gestured towards his pocket and I reached in to grab it. "Turn to the Forest of Demeter section," he said. I flipped through the pages. "Keep going," he added. I got to a page on forest fairies and held it up for him to read. "They are rumored to live in the treetops of the forest. They are knowledgeable creatures. Maybe they would know how to get the gloves off. Of course, you will have to go up to the tree tops yourself to ask," he said, holding up his gloved hands.

"Uh, ok. So I just fly up there and pop in like, 'Hello everyone. I'm just here to demand answers'," I asked, cocking an eyebrow. I was standing with my hands on my hips, tilting my head up to face him because he was so tall.

"That does sound like you, but I would not recommend it," he said, tossing back some sarcasm. "I would approach it like I would the gods or the earth. Be respectful, which will probably be difficult for you, but try your best. Ask them if they would be willing to help. It doesn't hurt to ask," he said, then shrugged.

"Sounds too easy," I said skeptically.

"Ok, you're right. Let's just continue on with my hands gloved and see what peril may befall us then," he said, sarcastically.

"You know, you act all sweet but you're kind of a brat deep down," I said, cocking my head to one side and smiling.

He shrugged, then huffed. He started walking again. We walked for a while, and the sky began to glow pink with the sunrise.

"Ok, I'll do the Friendly Fairy thing," I said, blowing out a breath and looking upward.

"Forest fairy," he corrected. He looked at me like he wasn't sure if I was kidding or not.

"Yeah, that's what I said," I replied, with an annoyed expression playing on my face.

I closed my eyes, readying to call on the gods for magic.

"At least I am able to hide what a brat I am. You just exude rudeness," he said, smiling. I had opened my eyes during his interruption.

"Shut up, I am trying to concentrate," I said. He laughed lightly, and I closed my eyes again. I extended my arms straight out to each side, palms up. I started to rise to the treetops, slowly. Once I got there, I was placed gently on a high branch overlooking the forest.

There were green tree tops for as far as I could see. How was I to look for a Forever Fairy, or whatever it was called, if I didn't even know what I was looking for? I blew out a breath looking around.

I called on the gods, closing my eyes. "Gaia, goddess of earth, present a Fairy to me that possesses answers so that I may help my friend," I whispered. "Please," I added, hoping it would make a difference.

I heard a buzzing, and my eyes snapped open. A tiny insect flew in front of my face. It looked like a dragonfly but with the body of a Fae. I held out my hand and it landed there. Its small body was clothed in green and belted at the waist with a black strip no larger than a piece of yarn. The Forest Fairy had short, dark purple hair and stood with its arms crossed. It looked perturbed and stood with one foot out in front of the other with brown pointed shoes.

"Is there a reason I was summoned?" The Forest Fairy asked in a small voice, raising her chin.

"Yes, I…" I stuttered then cleared my throat. "I have a problem that I was hoping you could help me with. I am not sure how to properly address you or what the procedures are here," I said nervously.

"Quinn," she said, bluntly. "My name is Quinn," she added, annoyed. She rolled her eyes and started tapping her foot.

"Quinn, it's a pleasure to mee-" I started but she cut me off.

"What do you want?" she interjected. "I don't have all day," she added.

"Well, my friend has magic binding gloves on and-," I started again.

"Oh, so you think I want to help you get them off?" she snapped. "Do you think I just sit around the forest all day waiting to save some damsel in distress and her idiot friend?" she asked.

Well, we agreed on one thing there. Lucas was an idiot sometimes. But he was my idiot, and my idiot needed saving. "I hoped that you would tell me how to get them off," I got out, finally. I was trying not to make my frustration visible, but she was being a real bitch.

"And what do I get in return?" she asked. She still stood there with her arms crossed. She had a terrible attitude. She was definitely not a friendly fairy.

I hadn't really thought about that. I didn't know what to offer her. "What would you seek for payment?" I asked, knowing I had nothing to give her.

"I want a home," she said, arms still crossed, one foot in front of the other.

"Well, I don't have any way to pay for such things," I said, breaking our eye contact.

"Who would you pay? We are in the middle of a forest. So stupid," she muttered the last two words and rolled her eyes again. "If you possess earth magic, you can make me one," she said. "And I already know that you do. I can sense it," she stated, lifting her chin.

"Sure, yeah, I can make you a home. Can you describe it to me?" I asked. I didn't really even know where to begin building a forest fairy home. She fluttered into the air.

"I want a hive made of hardened dirt with many holes in the sides leading in and out. I also want it to be protected by a protection spell so my family may safely live inside," she said, eyes narrowing.

"Ok," I said. "I can do that," I added. I closed my eyes and lifted my hands, palms facing out. I pictured what she had asked of me and gave a silent plea to the gods. I opened my eyes, and there it was, just as I had imagined it. I held my hand out for her to land in again. She had a smile on her face and no longer had her arms crossed as she landed. She squealed excitedly, bringing her tiny hands up to cover her mouth. She started jumping up and down, and glittering dust fell off of her.

"Now the protection spell," she said, turning to me. I must've looked confused because she rolled her eyes and sighed. "'Protego' The protection spell," she said, looking at me like I was an idiot.

I held my hand out towards her new dwelling, palm out, and

whispered, "Protego." The home lit up purple and then faded away. She smiled again.

"Ok, Legatum," she began. There was that word again that the mermaid had called me. "To unbind the gloves, you can use two different commands. The first, 'removere' will remove the binds. The other is 'vicissim' which will undo a spell," she said. Removere sounded familiar. I remembered Silas using that spell to remove my magic binding gloves.

"Ok, removere or vicissim. What was the other word you said?" I asked, confused.

"I said many words," she said, rolling her eyes with her arms crossed. She did that a lot. "You have all of the information you need," she said, then she shot away quickly.

I stood on the branch near her new home, but she had disappeared. I was high in the air, higher than I'd ever been, standing on a long pine branch, when I saw something move out of my peripheral. A giant beast was stalking toward me on an adjacent branch of a nearby tree. It had a tiger's body but thin glowing green stripes running up and down its body. The branch sagged under its weight.

I tried to keep a clear head and avoid panic. Lucas had told me a spell to kill a beast, but I couldn't recall the word right now. It took one more step in my direction, and, almost on instinct, my hand shot up, and lightning shot from my palm. It struck the branch the beast was on and the branch cracked. The beast plummeted toward the ground. After several moments I heard the thud of the beast. I descended quickly on the wind to return to Lucas.

I found Lucas propped up against a tree asleep just a few trees over. Or dead, but probably asleep. "Lucas," I said anxiously. I shoved him. He snored, confirming he wasn't dead. The beast lay still on the ground, but I couldn't be sure if it was dead or not.

"Lucas, seriously? Wake the fuck up," I whispered, pushing him. How had he slept through this giant beast falling from the sky?

He was sleeping deeply, so I decided to just cast the spells on him hastily. I knelt in front of him and sat on my knees. I glanced over at the beast, still lying there unmoving. I held my hands up in front of me, palms pointing at Lucas. "Removere," I breathed, with a roll of my tongue.

The gloves were instantly gone, along with all of Lucas' clothes. Whoops. Lucas slowly started to wake and looked down at his naked body. He propped himself up on his elbows, not cowering, with his body completely exposed to me. I shook my head.

He was clearly very comfortable in his skin and didn't seem bothered at all by lying naked in front of me. My eyes fell as low as his toned abs before turning away quickly. Gross.

"Evie, if you wanted to see me naked so badly, you could've just asked," he said with an amused tone.

I held my finger up to my mouth with widened eyes. I glanced over my shoulder to check the beast. It was still lying on the ground in a large lump. "Gross, put some clothes on," I whispered, covering my eyes with my hand, as if disgusted. I pointed my free hand at his crotch and said, "Vicissim."

I peeked through my fingers that I was using to cover my eyes to see that he was wearing pants again.

"Can I have a shirt too or just pants?" he asked smiling. Clearly he thought this was hilarious. I pointed at his chest and said, "Vicissim." His shirt was back on his body, but the gloves were gone now. No chance of saving them to use on someone else.

"Look at you, Evie. Using spells and shit," he said. I choked a laugh.

"Lucas!" I exclaimed, shushing him. I looked over my shoulder to see the beast rising to its feet. I lifted my hands, creating an orb around us made of air. I added static to it, and it crackled and glowed. Purple ebbed and flowed across it, as I offered the gods a silent plea to protect us. I was impressive when I was under pressure.

The beast pushed up onto all fours and looked around. I crouched under the dome, not really sure what I was able to do. The animal saw me and snarled. I couldn't tell if it saw the dome around us or not before it leapt into the air. The beast landed hard on the dome, shaking it, but the dome held strong. I internally asked the gods to continue to lend me their power. The beast did not puncture the dome. In fact, it seemed repelled. It jumped off the dome and took off running in the opposite direction.

I realized I was crouched on the ground, palms pointing up and out. Lucas was crouched too, with wide eyes and a smile crept across his face.

"Holy shit, Evie," he said. "That took a lot of power," he added, surprised.

"The problem is, I feel like I perform better under pressure. I can't just will it at any time," I added, frowning. The dome started to melt away, returning to the earth.

"It's better to work under pressure than not at all," Lucas said with a shrug. I guessed he was right. I just wished I could always call to it.

"Can you recall your thoughts when you harness your elements?" he asked, standing to his full height. The dome was completely gone now.

"Usually, I am in a complete panic. Internally, I am begging the gods to borrow their power," I recalled.

"Maybe it's because you are humbled and drop your tough Fae

act," he said, arching a brow.

"Oh shut up, Lucas. It's not an act," I said, pursing my lips. Lucas pinched his brows, not believing me. In response, I barked a laugh. "Ok, asshole. Maybe you have a point. I get it," I said, rolling my eyes. I yawned. After my adrenaline settled and realizing that Lucas was free now, the fatigue was overwhelming. "I am so tired, Lucas," I said through my yawn.

"Why don't you lay down here and take a nap, and I will stand guard," he suggested.

Lenore layed down right where we were talking as if she wanted a nap as well. She had run all night, after all. I smiled at her and pet her neck.

"I would love that," I said. I didn't even have the energy for a sarcastic comment. I sat right where I had been standing, and I swear I was asleep before my head hit the grass.

A male stood before me, but I couldn't see his face. "Evie," he said urgently. "You must be careful when you visit the Oracle today," he continued. A vision flashed before me of a clearing with a cave that had light blue light emitting from it. It looked as though the inside of the cave was glowing. Awareness flooded my mind, and I knew the Oracle was housed there. "When you exit, Silas will be waiting. Be prepared to fight," he said. Then I saw a vision of me, lying on my back in the grass. Silas knelt above me with a knife drawn in the air. He plunged the blade down into my heart.

I awoke with a jolt and shot up to a sitting position, gasping for breath. It had been a bad dream. Lucas looked at me in shock from where he sat beside me in the grass. Lenore raised up from where she had been sleeping as well. She stood like she was ready to carry me to safety if I needed it.

"I had a dream about finding the Oracle," I said between breaths. "A male showed me the cave the Oracle is in and said I have to go today. I think I can get us there by Pega-travel," I said, pausing to wet my mouth.

"Evie, it was just a bad dream," he said, trying to calm me.

"I get messages on the wind from someone. They've always helped me along," I said.

"This vision may not have anything to do with your messages on the wind. This was a dream, which would require a different sort of magic than harnessing the air," he said, having a valid point. "Honestly, it could be a trap they are laying for you," he added.

"The male warned me that Silas would be waiting for me when I exited the cave. He showed me my death. In the vision, Silas stood over me and stabbed me in the heart with a knife," I said, my chest rising and falling quickly. "Why would I get the warning if it was a trap?" I asked.

Lucas paused for a moment. "Ok, so let's say we go. You find the Oracle, you get your power ring, and everything is perfect, yeah?" he asked sarcastically. "Then you exit the cave and kiss your ass goodbye," he said, putting his finger to his chin and tapping it. He pushed his lips out and looked to the side, mock thinking.

"Listen, idiot, obviously, I am not just going to walk out of the cave into Silas' hands. I thought maybe we could devise a plan," I said, putting my hands on my hips. I squinted at him, "Unless you want me to walk out and be stabbed." A smile crept across my face.

He laughed deeply. "Ok, so what's the plan for exiting the cave then?" he asked.

"Why don't we just not exit?" I asked.

"Oh ok, we will just live there forever," he said mockingly, nodding his head excitedly.

"Or Pega-travel out," I said.

"Ok, good first plan. We need a backup plan. I have heard that the Oracle doesn't let Fae travel in and out of her cave magically because it can be dangerous for her," he said.

"Ok, good point." I thought about it some more. I held out my palm. I thought of the earth giving me the iron needed to create a blade. I imagined a wooden handle made from the trees. I thought about the pieces forming together to create a beautiful weapon gifted from the earth. I opened my eyes to see that I had willed a knife into my hand. It was similar to the weapon the gods had given me to save Lenore. Maybe the gods would just save me from this fate too.

"Nice," Lucas said. "But we can't take weapons into the cave. Oracle's rules," he said, then shrugged.

"Ok, what if before we enter, we start a small fire that builds while we're with the Oracle," I started. "Then, after we see her, we run out of the cave as fast as we can until we can cast magic again, the fire will be a distraction. Then we Pega-travel back to the Academy," I finished. I looked up from my absorption to meet Lucas' eyes.

"What if we go to exit the cave, and they have already put the fire out?" Lucas asked, trying to prepare for the worst.

"Ok, scratch the fire. What if we cause a bad storm before entering the cave?" I said, thinking aloud.

"And when we exit, we get struck by lightning," Lucas interjected.

I dropped my arms to my sides, clapping against my thighs. "I don't know, Lucas. I just know we have to go today," I said and lifted a hand to rub my temple.

"Maybe you could ask the Oracle how to get away when you're with her," Lucas said and shrugged.

That wasn't a terrible idea. "What if she won't offer help to me?" I asked.

"Then you can kiss your pretty little ass goodbye," he said. "Before you leave the cave," he added and smiled as if we weren't discussing my death.

I took a moment to think, rubbing my palms over my eyes. "Well, in the vision, I was laying way off to the right of the cave. So, when we exit, we run left," I offered.

"What if that's a trap?" He asked.

"What if it's not?" I asked. Lucas blew out a breath.

"Ok, you lead and I'll follow," he said, not looking convinced.

I stood up, walked towards Lenore, and ran my hand down her neck. "You'll be ok, girl. I will be back for you as soon as possible," I said sadly. I held out my hand, palm facing the ground. I used my earth magic to grow a massive bush of blueberries. Lenore pounced on them like a cat, and I smiled.

"Protego," I breathed on her neck. I remembered the protection spell the forest fairy had taught me and hoped it would be enough to keep Lenore safe until I returned for her.

"Shall we go then?" I asked, offering my elbow to Lucas. He blew out a breath and reached into his pocket. He plucked out a Pegasus feather, looping his arm in mine.

I took a deep breath, "In case I die, I just want to say thanks for everything," I blurted. Then continued, "And," I swallowed, "I love you." He burst out laughing. "Like a brother, you idiot," I added, rolling my eyes. "You are actually becoming quite an asshole," I said, smiling.

"You're not going to die, idiot," he said, sweetly. He held the feather out in front of me. Most people balked at the way I talked or were intimidated. Lucas just gave it right back to me. Who knew we would become so close, so fast?

I closed my eyes. I cleared my mind and attempted to focus. I wasn't nervous, just excited. Ok, I was a little nervous. I needed to concentrate on transporting us to the cave using the Pegasus feather. I would have to light the feather and give the command for where we were going since the image of the cave was in my head. I held up the palm of my free arm. I cast a flame in my palm that traveled to the tip of my pointer finger. I opened my mouth to speak, but Lucas spoke first.

"I love you too, Evie," he said and I smiled.

"To the cave of the Oracle of Isla," I said, concentrating on the image I had been gifted in my dream. I opened my eyes preparing to travel.

With a clap of magic, the world blinked out of existence and when it came back into view again, we stood a way off from a large cave.

Chapter 18

The cave looked precisely like the image that I had been gifted. There was one entrance and it glowed a bright blue. It was made of stone and was cut into the side of a hill. A traveler could have easily overlooked it; it was a great place to hide. Continuing down the hillside was a river. A dirt path lined with trees sat between the river and the cave. The cave mouth was blocked from view by the trees, but past the trees was a clearing leading up to the mouth of the cave.

Lucas and I were still arm in arm. I slid my arm out of his and placed both arms at my sides. "Do we just walk in?" I asked Lucas, turning to face him.

"When we approach, we will have to ask permission to be able to enter," he said. "You will state your name and why you're here. Remember, be respectful," he said with a smile and raised brows like he wasn't sure I could be respectful. He bumped into me with his hip forcing me to take a step to catch myself.

I rolled my eyes and started walking toward the cave entrance. He was always one step behind me or directly beside me, never letting me face anything alone. I loved him for that.

We approached the entrance, and the blue glow increased. Lucas elbowed me in the ribs lightly. I cleared my throat. He nodded in encouragement.

"I am Evelyn Warren of the Kingdom of Aether. I am twenty-one and have come to receive my power ring," I said, trying to ensure I didn't forget anything.

The glow disappeared, and I guessed that meant we could enter. I was frozen in place, deep in thought. Lucas laced his fingers in between mine and started to walk. I still had the knife from earlier, and not wanting to offend the Oracle, I grabbed it out of my pocket. I tossed it aside, not paying attention to where it landed.

Since the glow was gone I couldn't see anything. I wasn't sure there was even a floor going forward. Perhaps, we were about to plunge into a bottomless pit. Lucas pushed me along.

A line of lights lit up on the floor leading us down, what I could now tell, was a curved stone hallway. Lucas' head almost touched the ceiling because he was stupidly tall.

The hallway got narrower, and we could no longer walk side by side. Lucas bent down to speak into my ear. "Go ahead, Evie. I will be right behind you. You're safe," he whispered reassuringly.

"Don't let go of my hand. I will let go when I feel sure it's safe," I said, knowing he wouldn't make fun of me for being a huge baby at a time like this.

"Of course," he bent forward and whispered. I stepped in front of him to continue down the hallway. My arm was stretched behind me to hold his.

The hallway sloped slightly downward, still curving, and I wondered how deep into the cave we would have to go. I also felt like it was getting narrower. I wondered if my huge muscular friend would be able to travel the whole way. My hands felt sweaty, and the anticipation was killing me.

The hallway was curving to the right and finally broke open into a large room. The room was stone on all sides with a high ceiling.

"Evie, I should wait here. If I go in with you, she may not reveal things to you," he said. "But I promise, I will be right here when you're through," he said and I believed him. I nodded and let go of his hand, stepping into the room.

I walked into an enormous, beautiful cavern. Flames were dancing around up towards the ceiling showing off a beautiful, colorful display. The cavern ceiling glimmered with precious stones that protruded unevenly.

In the middle of the room was a stone table that looked like an altar. I wondered where the Oracle was. Behind the altar, smoke started to faintly grow. Rising from the floor, as if made of smoke herself, a beautiful female formed out of blue vapor. She was stunning. She had pale, smooth skin and a thin, lithe body. She looked no older than me, even though the legend said she was over five hundred years old. She had long, straight red hair pulled back at the base of her head. She had a gold band across her forehead and large green eyes that made her look approachable and warm.

"Legatum, you have come. I was unsure of whether we would meet or not, not knowing if I was needed," she purred. "The lost heir. Oh and you have met your mate, I see. Did you come to ask me about his nature? He too can harness the darkness," she added. I was overwhelmed with all the revelations.

She didn't think I would come? Why wouldn't I come? This was now the third creature to call me Legatum, what was with that? And what was that? Did they have me confused for someone else? And I hadn't met my mate. It sure as hell wasn't Lucas.

"I have come for my power ring. My name is Evelyn," I stated. I was confused about all the misinformation I was receiving from the Oracle. She was supposed to be all-knowing.

"I know who you are, Legatum. Have you yet realized that you possess the power to harness all elements, including the element of darkness?" she purred.

"My name is Evelyn, not Legatum. I did realize I can harness light, air, water, and earth but I didn't know about darkness," I said, slightly concerned.

"You are one of four who possessed all five elemental affinities," she purred. "Actually, there is a fifth, your mate. Unless you deny him," she added.

I was shocked and confused. I shifted my weight from one hip to the other. I tried to remember how to form words. I wanted to ask why I could harness darkness, but I was so blindsided by her revelations that I wasn't prepared.

"Legatum, hold out your right hand," I did as she asked, still not understanding what Legatum meant.

She pulled a piece of hair from her scalp and looped it around the middle finger of my right hand three times. She closed her eyes and placed one hand above mine and one below without making contact. Her hands were thin and delicate. "Close your eyes, Legatum," she directed. I did as she asked and heard her whisper, "Encapsulate elementum virtutis."

Magic clapped loudly, and my finger burned. I opened my eyes and looked down to see a silver ring on my finger. It was beautiful, with a large circle on top. The circle was a beautiful, swirling purple. Five small circles were attached to the main circle: white for air, blue for water, yellow for light, green for earth, and black for darkness. I swallowed when I noticed the black stone.

"Why can I harness darkness?" I finally choked out.

"Why wouldn't you?" she said and cocked her head. She slowed contemplatively. "Oh, you do not know?" she asked.

I shook my head no. "Know what?" I inquired.

"It is not mine to reveal," she said, emotionless. "You must seek the source," she added. I thought she was the source that explained all the answers.

"If I don't know what I don't know, how will I know the source?" I asked, confused. Anyone that could be helpful to me spoke in ways that I couldn't understand. It was really getting frustrating. There was obviously a great secret around who I was and who my parents were, but if no one would tell me, how I would ever find out.

"Well that is the great mystery, Legatum. I do not know why you do not know. It is a mystery to me as well, for it is not for me to know," she said. "You have quite the quest ahead of you," she added.

I rubbed my forehead with my fingers. What the fuck was she even saying right now?

"You must seek the source for answers," she added again. That piece of information made no sense. I didn't know who or what the source could be.

"Why did you seem surprised that I came here?" I asked.

"You came for a power ring to replenish your power, but your power never depletes, so I am unsure as to why you visited me," she said.

"Why doesn't my power deplete like other Fae?" I asked.

"That is a part of your quest for answers. You must not dally," she said. "It was a pleasure, Legatum," and she started to turn to blue vapor just like she had entered.

"Wait!" I blurted. "A male seeks to murder me outside of this cave. Please tell me how to escape him," I said as she disappeared into smoke.

Suddenly, the wind caressed my ear and spoke a single word. "Fly," Isla's voice purred.

Chapter 19

I walked back the way I had come. I only took a few steps into the room to approach the altar so I turned on my heel and headed back to Lucas. Isla had evaporated. "Holy shit," I said, feeling nauseous. "Shit, shit, shit," I said, forming both of my hands into fists. I had closed the distance between Lucas and me. "I wanted to ask her what my shifted form is, but she wasn't really giving me a lot of information," I said to Lucas.

"We will figure that out later. It's time to escape your death," he said, smiling.

"Why do you look so excited about the prospect of me dying?" I asked, cocking my head and pouting my lips.

"You're not going to die, Evie," Lucas reassured me.

We quickly headed up the path back to the cave entrance. I followed Lucas until the trail widened and joined him at his side. I was starting to feel nervous. I had never faced the threat of death, knowing it beforehand. I also felt excited too. I had always lived for the thrill. I just wondered if I was powerful enough yet to fight off a trained Fae like Silas. I knew I would be a force to be reckoned with in time, but I was still learning.

As the outside light got brighter, I slowed. We couldn't use magic inside the cave, so we needed to start running to the left. I started going over the plan with Lucas, when the knife I had dropped outside the cave caught my eye. Should I risk retrieving the knife by heading towards my death? Maybe that was the knife Silas was going to stab me with. No, something in my gut told me not to go that way. I decided to stick to the plan and run left.

"What if I can't get my wings to come out?" I asked Lucas. I had only done it once and failed the second time I tried.

"If you can't shift, jump on my back and we will ride off together," Lucas said. I nodded in agreement. "You can do this, Evie. Be confident. Ready?" he said, a gleam in his eye. He must live for danger or something. Then again, he wasn't the one that was going to get stabbed. I smiled nervously.

"Go," I said quickly, and we ran out of the cave, heading north. As we ran, my eyes adjusted from the cave's darkness to the bright sun outside. The terrain was smooth and was covered in grass. We sped across it easily. I plowed forward putting one foot in front of the other as fast as I possibly could. We veered to the left, and there was no one in sight. I was apprehensive because this seemed too easy. I kept pushing forward, one foot pounding in front of the other.

In an instant, Silas and his guards ran out from around the right side of the cave. Some headed up the grassy side of the hill, to stand at the top of the cave while some ran after us. I could see males flanking Silas on either side. Arrows started zooming past us. I threw my hands up over my head but kept running. I willed my huge, white wings to burst from my back. As they emerged, I tipped forwards to try to adjust to their weight. I found my balance again and I started flapping while running.

I heard a grunt and dared a glance over my shoulder to find Lucas, in his shifted form, laying on the ground, struggling. He had an arrow sticking out of his eagle feathers and he was furiously trying to push himself up into a standing position when another arrow struck him. The first arrow was sticking out of his left side, and was tied to a rope. The rope was attached to a huge boulder, and two guards were pulling on the rope. It must've jerked him backwards when the rope ran out of slack, throwing him to the ground. Even once he pushed himself back into a standing position, he would still be attached to a boulder.

"Lucas!" I screamed, turning back towards him with a skid. My knees strained at the sudden shift in plans.

I acted fast and with confidence. I traced the arrows' flight back to the top of the cliff. I held my palm up, and shot a burst of air knocking the males standing there back onto their asses. Jake was the only one left standing. His hair blew lightly in the breeze, and he stood with a bow and arrow pointed at the ground. He had a half-smile on his face. What was with that guy? The three guards behind him were scrambling to a standing position.

I ran back for my friend and, palm aimed at the rope with my other hand, willed fire into existence. I threw a palm up towards Silas and his two guards and blasted them with air magic to buy myself some time. The three of them flew back. The rope was burning, severing the tie pinning Lucas to the boulder. Lucas climbed up into a standing position and yanked the arrow from his side with a wince. As he grabbed the other arrow, I breathed, "Sana," healing his wounds. A bead of blood ran down his side but it had stopped flowing from the wound. Lucas started moving forward again. I waited for Lucas to catch up to me, holding out my hand. Once he grabbed my hand, we turned and began running again. I could hear the guards returning to their feet, and arrows had started pinging off of the rocks around us again. I threw my hands up over my shoulder and willed fire to shoot out of them. I didn't know where it landed or if it hit anyone and I didn't dare risk a look back. We had to get out of here. I could hear Silas and the guards scrambling towards us too.

We broke apart to accommodate our wingspans. Beating our wings, we leapt into the air and lifted off the ground. We beat our wings hard and rose higher and higher. I turned and saw Silas loading another arrow into his bow. I aimed my hand at him, and shot more air in his direction.

Once in the air, I spoke to the wind, "Why do I always have to save your ass?" and sent it to Lucas. I knew when the message reached him because he cawed. The wind swept my long hair behind me. The sun was still shining and the freedom of the wind was filling me with warmth. I felt like I had escaped death.

A debilitating, sharp pain shot through my side and I sucked in a breath. I clutched my side and took a shallow breath. My wings seized mid-flight. I felt myself start to fall from the sky. Time slowed and I looked down at my side in slow motion. I saw the knife I had left outside of the cave sticking out of my side. I was void of energy and I could not will my wings to beat. My eyes were heavy and my body started to fall backward. Lucas' wings started to flap backward in a panic. I felt the breeze catch me and cradle me, preventing me from falling. I felt like I was laying on my back high in the air. I slowly grabbed the knife with both hands and clenched my teeth. I pulled the knife from my side and clutched the gaping wound underneath. Blood started to spew from my side.

Lucas was now under me lifting my weight off my bed on the breeze. Everything was still moving in slow motion when a message reached my ear. I knew it didn't come from Lucas because his mouth hadn't moved, and it wasn't his voice.

"Sana," the familiar male voice said into my ear. The pain ebbed away, and I looked down to see the wound, glowing green, begin to close. I felt my energy returning to me and spreading through my body. I felt my strength again, and determination fueled me. I landed on Lucas' back and time returned to its normal speed suddenly, disorienting me. I started beating my wings while still on Lucas' back. I knew we could travel faster if he didn't have to carry me. I was finally able to carry my weight again and flew off of Lucas' back. He returned to my side, and we beat our wings hard to propel ourselves through the sky. The ground was getting further and further, and my adrenaline was pulsing through my body.

I risked a look back. Jake still stood on top of the hill a good ways away from Silas. His gaze locked on me. His bow had an arrow knocked, but it was still pointing at the ground. His mouth was moving but I didn't hear his shouts. Maybe he was cursing himself under his breath? He didn't look mad though, he looked satisfied. I turned to face forward again.

Another message found me on the wind. "Well done, Evie. Return to a safe place. Bad news awaits you," the gentle caress landed on my ear. The voice was that of the male who had helped me all along. I tried to calm my pounding heart and I was filled with dread.

I yelled to Lucas, "We need to land. We have to Pega-travel back to the Academy." I hoped everything was ok with Jude.

We glided over the treetops, slowing our flapping until we saw a hill with a clearing that was safe to land in. Lucas yelled to me and pointed, "There." We came in for a swift landing and I beat my wings backward to slow myself. This was only my second landing and my first landing had been rough. I flapped in place and slowly lowered myself, like I had watched Silas' guard and Lucas do, until my feet were touching the rock and I had my balance. Then, I held my wings straight out to balance myself and folded them in when I was steady. Much better.

Once we were both landed, I turned to Lucas, breathless. "Something bad has happened," I started to say. I tried to catch my breath. I swallowed to wet my mouth. "The voice told me on the wind. We need to go back to the Academy and meet Jude," I said, hands on my hips.

"I would feel better if we knew who 'the voice' was," Lucas said with a frown. "I just hope it's not gaining our trust, just to set us up in the end," he said. I didn't know how to explain it, but I trusted the voice. I had also trusted Silas, briefly, so maybe it was good to have someone call me out on my bullshit.

"I don't know, Lucas. Why bring us this far just to end us? The voice could've ended me, and especially your dumb ass, a long time ago," I said and he smiled in response. I stood there for a moment, my hands on my hips while I tried to catch my breath.

Lucas pulled out a Pegasus feather and we looped arms, familiar with Pega-travel. I cast fire in my palm and held the flame up to the feather. "The Academy of Athena," I commanded.

And with a clap of magic, we were gone.

About The Author

J. J. Smeck

J. J. Smeck has a Master's Degree in Education and enjoys writing Fantasy novels. She is a special education teacher, a mother of three, and a devoted wife. More importantly, she enjoys smut and wine.

The Kingdom of Chaos is a three book series taking place in the royal Kingdom of Chaos. If that isn't enough, there are two more three book series that take place in the same fantasy world, the Kingdom of Chaos, that J. J. created.

Follow J. J. on instagram @j.j.smeck for upcoming release dates.

Books In This Series

The Kingdom of Chaos

Book 1: The Kingdom of Chaos: Becoming Fae
Book 2: The Kingdom of Chaos: Accepting Fate (9/2022)
Book 3: The Kingdom of Chaos: the Lost Kingdom's Uprising (11/2022)

Book 4: The Kingdom of Chaos: Restoring the Royal Kingdom (2023)
Book 5: The Kingdom of Chaos: The Kingdom of the Saved (2023)
Book 6: The Kingdom of Chaos: A Kingdom Crumbles (2023)

Book 7: The Kingdom of Chaos: Reparations (2024)
Book 8: The Kingdom of Chaos: Discord (2024)
Book 9: The Kingdom of Chaos: Redemption (2024)

The Kingdom Of Chaos: Becoming Fae

Every Fae in the royal Kingdom of Chaos looks forward to receiving their power ring on their twenty-first birthday to refuel their elemental affinities. Evie wakes up to find herself imprisoned instead. She soon finds out that the life she thought she had is not actually the one she was meant to live. The more she seeks the truth, the further she gets from finding it.

Made in United States
North Haven, CT
11 July 2022